My Lover From The Star Planet

Teerinthorn Watchman

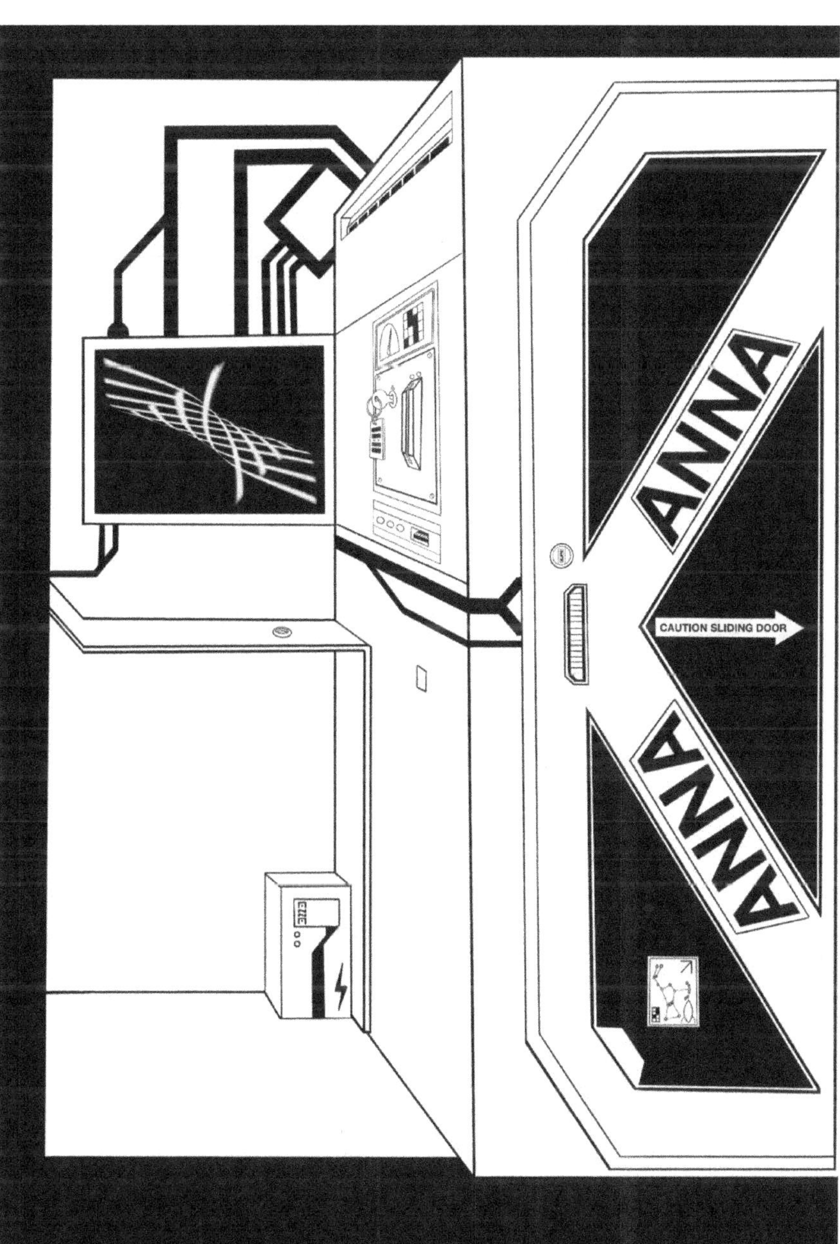

ANNA
CAUTION SLIDING DOOR
ANNA

CONTENTS

ACKNOWLEDGMENTS

I would like to thank my husband, Eric. 'Your love of the Star people inspired me to write this story.' Also my mother-in-law, the smartest woman I have ever met, who helped me sort out my grammatical dilemma and Hinano, my daughter who made my characters sassier than they were. Lastly, I love you, dad for encouraging me and teaching me to write

CHAPTER ONE: MY FIRST ENCOUNTER

Do aliens really exist? There is so much proof, so many witnesses, so many encounters yet...any known cases of aliens are still a mystery to humans.'

———————————————————————————————-

"Gender equality!"

"Stop workplace bullying!"

"More women in the executive suite please!"

Multiple feminists representing the female rights movement demonstrated on the streets, signs in hand. Sia, a young female with ebony hair and brown eyes, an Asian gene she received from her father, began to yell, "Stop workplace bullying!" She wasn't really doing this for any righteous reason than to get on her father's nerves. It's not that she doesn't like her father. Rather she doesn't like her adopted brother, Luke. All her bad luck seemed to have sprouted 11 years ago ever since her father had first adopted him. Luke has been working full time for David Young, her father, since graduating university. For her father believes the highest form of loyalty comes from familial ties, adopting Luke satisfied David enough grant to give Luke a bigger role in the company. The problem is, Sia hates Luke, and for good reason.

Employees who have worked under him all gossip about how he always takes credit from other's work and claims it as his own. Her father doesn't listen to any of those complaints. He always says, "As long as he gets the job done, I don't care how he does it."

Sia's family hotel business started with her grandfather. When Sia's grandfather died, David Young took over his father's business. He currently owns multiple hotels in the small state of New Mexico. Even before his career, Luke had always been working odd jobs for the Youngs since middle school. Sia agrees that one thing going for Luke is his determination. He lived near her house as a young teen and he often came by, ringing her doorbell and asking to work on her front yard. Her dad loved Luke's personality. His keen demeanor and desire to rise up in society appealed to Sia's father greatly. For $20 a week, Luke was hired to mow the lawn. When Luke found out that her father was a successful businessman, he asked to work as an intern at one of the Young's hotels while he pursued his bachelor's degree in business and tourism. Her father has always loved Luke. He even tried to get Sia to go out on a date with him. Luckily, Luke had no interest in women which Sia always thought was obvious but not to her father. Although there were many reasons, this, in particular, was one of the main reasons they never hooked up.

Now instead of becoming a lover, Luke secretly became Sia's adversary, often making her look like a lazy and spoiled child to her father.

"Sia! What has gotten into you, yelling in front of the hotel like that?" Her father scorns her actions, before sending a security guard to drag her into his office. "If you have that much time, you should at least start working for the business. Luke's not even my son by blood, yet he acts more like my child than you. He works hard every single day, almost single-handedly keeping our company alive. You are my biological child but you just act like you don't care. All you know how to do is spend my money and cause trouble." David begins to shout.

"Yeah, yeah...Luke is just the best! He's the greatest son any father could have, blah, blah, blah," Sia mocks, "You have him working for you already, what do you still need me for? Hm?" Sia argues before walking out of her dad's office.

"Sia, you-!" David is shaking his finger at her knowing there was nothing more he could say. He usually doesn't like his employees witnessing him and Sia arguing and She knows this well. Of course, the arguing will most definitely continue once her father arrives home tonight. So when Sia's good friend Nadia, invited her to a Masquerade party at a popular high-class hotel near downtown Sia accepted her invitation right away.

"I heard the owner of the hotel, Eli, is ridiculously handsome! Almost like an ancient Greek god! Oh my, I hope the rumors are true..." Nadia purrs, her already shrill voice becoming higher as she twirls her hair.

"Can't you just google him?" Sia asks.

"Trust me, I've tried. I guess he doesn't like having his photo taken," Nadia shrugs, "In fact, he hardly promotes his hotel anywhere but his business is doing so... well. Isn't that weird? There's even a three-month waiting list to book his hotel! Can you believe that? It's not like other hotels where you can just... you know, walk-in."

"Impressive," Sia answers nonchalantly. Maybe the long waiting list is because there aren't many rooms to begin with.

However, after arriving at Eli's hotel, Sia immediately knew she was wrong. The hotel is quite big, probably even one of the biggest hotels in Downtown. Sia hardly drives through Downtown because of all the traffic and the lack of public parking so she had never noticed Eli's hotel before until now.

The parking lots were packed but the hotel had its own parking lot underneath, which is especially convenient for the guests. Surprisingly, the guests' vehicles are mostly high-ended brands like Benz, BMW, Tesla. There are even electronic charging stations for the visitors in the parking lot, Sia thinks this is very unique and perhaps admirable. This type of service is rare in a small state like New Mexico. Despite that, this is the first time she has seen so many expensive cars parked in the same parking lot. Well, other than a car showroom of course. These aren't your average tourists.

Nadia acted as if she grew up in this hotel, leading Sia to an elevator. "Since the best view of Downtown can be seen here at sundown, we're going all the way up, girl!" Nadia exclaims with a glimmer in her eye.

Once they made their way to the top of the building, looking around, it appears to be a dome with glossy glass walls surrounding a party of masked guests dressed to perfection with gleeful smiles. With more women than men, Sia is met with a strong whiff of perfume when she enters the hall. Although Nadia warned her, Sia regrets not dressing nicer.

"What do you think? Nice, isn't it?"

"Sure," Sia answers abruptly. "Um, I need to use the restroom. You know where it is?"

"I think I've seen a sign near the elevator." Nadia waves in that general direction before disappearing into the crowd

"Thanks, I'll be back in a minute" Sia answers, walking out of the glass room. However, there are quite a few people already waiting so Sia decides to take the stairs and use the restroom on the floor below. Usually, most business buildings have the same floor plan for the restroom on every floor. At least every floor should have a restroom...

Sia's guess is right. After descending the stairwell, she sees a brightly lit restroom sign. The layout of this floor is a bit different from the top floor. There are rooms after rooms, sort of like an office space.

"This may be the main office space for the hotel," She hums, "But where is everybody?" Curiosity begins to set in.

Upon leaving the restroom, She continues down the hall. "Nice office space." She is amazed. It's almost like a home office. The windows are sheer glass and the employees are presented with a mountain vista, a view that would be stunning on a snowy day…

BAM

"Ah! sorry!" Sia yelps out loud, stumbling back after walking right into someone's chest.

A very tall, dark-haired young man looks at her with a surprised look, his deep-set green eyes seem to glimmer under the LED lights. His silence makes Sia nervous.

"I'm, uh, looking for a restroom. It's packed upstairs so…" She mumbles, tucking a lock of hair behind her ear.

He nods, pointing to a room behind her.

Before leaving, she asked, "Do you work here?"

"Yes." He answers in a normal voice, neither happy nor mad.

"A man of limited words." She says to herself. Interesting… perhaps a little weird.

Sia walks back to the restroom looking back to make sure he was gone before going past the restroom and heading back to the stairs.

The size of the party had increased since she left. Sia starts looking for Nadia and sees her friend speaking with a middle-aged man before her friend notices her.

"Hey, Sia, come this way!" Nadia waves her hands, "Where have you been? You know Eli Star arrived a few minutes ago. You just missed him

"Where is he?" Sia asks. Perhaps, he was the man she met downstairs, he was very handsome after all.

"He went backstage. He may come out later, I think." Nadia answers,

"Look! A bunch of girls just ran to the stage. Should we go too?" Nadia cannot keep her excitement down. Sia feels a tinge of embarrassment for her friend.

"You already have a boyfriend, why do you want to see him anyway? Did you already see his face?"

"He wore a mask but he is very tall and his body smells so... nice. It was like cologne but... not? It was very light yet noticeable if that makes sense. " Nadia closes her eyes, imaging his face underneath the mask. "He'll be my imaginary husband from now on." Nadia smiles coyly.

"Eww!" Sia teases as the pair began to laugh.

"Let's go! Wait for him over there." Nadia points at the stage. Sia let Nadia lead her again.

About 10 minutes later, Eli walks out on the stage, wearing a deep blue suit, his face disguised by a matching feather mask. Even so, Sia remembers right away that he was the same man she saw downstairs.

"Wait, I-I just saw him downstairs! Without the mask on!" Sia declares almost teasingly to her friend.

"What? No way! Wait, but why did you go downstairs?" Nadia says in disbelief.

"The restroom was full so I just went downstairs and he came out from his office, I guess."

"REALLY?" Nadia raises her voice unintentionally.

"Really!"

Nadia smirks, "So...is he really handsome like a Greek god?"

"Umm...I guess so. He didn't talk much and his eyes are a little cold but... he seemed interesting. I wouldn't go out with him personally. He looks scary, to be honest." Sia concludes, trying to declare her first impression of him.

The introduction music begins to play, both girls' eyes are focus on the stage. A host announces the name, the president of the Star hotel "Eli Star".

"Welcome everyone! Thank you very much for attending our yearly masquerade." Eli expresses, the guests are listening attentively. Sia starts to notice something unique about his guests tonight. Many of them could be considered prodigies and some are even well-known to the public, this explains why there are so many luxury cars in the parking lot. She has seen many of these people conduct business with her father a couple of times. Their masks didn't really cover their unique features, Sia really just needed to spend some time observing them and she will be able to put a name to those faces she recognizes.

Sia doesn't know what's so special about this party and why they all have to be here. It seemed normal but yet boring. No special entertainment nor special foods and beverages. Why are all these people here?

"Nadia..." Sia turns to her friend but Nadia has slipped out to flirt with a man at the balcony. She doesn't want to bother her friend so she decides to walk back to the hallway, just to admire the architecture of the hotel.

Sia loves the design of this hotel. No wonder people like to stay here, everything is made with lavish high-end materials. The art that decorated the hotel appeared lovingly handcrafted and is reminiscent of the distinct Native American artwork of the Southwest. She wanders aimlessly until she met another stairwell.

"What the ..." Her curiosity begins to run wild, "hmm, maybe I can check out Eli's office once more..." She is hoping to perhaps see Eli again and maybe this time she will introduce herself properly. He works in the same industry as her dad anyway. Maybe she can ask what was his secret to conducting such a successful hospitality business. If she can utilize some successful strategies with the family business, maybe her dad won't complain about her being "good for nothing" anymore.

Sia walks to the middle of office floor but this time, things are a lot different than before. The empty office from before is now full of people. Their masks were removed and she was right, many of the masked figures she recognized are the rich and intelligent people she had seen before either on television or at her father's hotel speaking to a conference. There are influential business people and highly regarded scholars.

"Why are they here?" Sia wonders. Her sense of security advises her not to show herself but to hide and watch them with caution.

"Eli…" Sia whispers to herself when the renowned owner joins his guests. He shakes the hands of every guest and some of them follows him to yet another big room. But it isn't an office space. It looked more like a lab of sorts. She is only able to see inside from the door as the walls appeared normal, unlike the glass walls of its surrounding rooms.

Minutes later, Eli, alone, walks out of the room to bring more people from the glass office to the lab. More people from the reception are now entering the glass office. At this point, Sia is sure they were here for the lab or something there.

"What is that lab for?" Although the room looks big, it is definitely too small to fit that many people. "What are they doing in there?" The only way she'll know is to go in there with those clowns. Holding the mask tight, Sia walks toward the group of guests who had just gotten on the floor through the main elevator. All the guests begin taking off their masks as they entered the glass office. She quickly follows suit and does her best to hide in a corner.

Good thing these people aren't speaking to one another. It seems as if they're trying their best to keep a low profile, almost like they're sneaking out of the party to enter the office peacefully.

Eli comes out again. He calls out five names and motions them to follow him. Once he turns his back, Sia hides amongst the group while everyone is focused on the lab entrance.

The sliding door of the lab is opened automatically and, surprisingly, no one is inside. Absolutely no one. There is only a gigantic machine in the middle of the room and five elevators with glass doors. Sia quietly slips away and ducks behind the machine which kind of looks like a standing controller. Eli turns to face the group and all the guests, one by one, walked toward the elevators. Then, Eli made his way to the controller, keying in something before pushing a button. The elevator doors closed and suddenly all the guests disappeared like magic, similar to a show Sia had seen when she was young.

"Oh! Oh my!" Sia cries loudly, instinctively using her hands to cover her mouth but it was already too late. Eli spins around to the source of the noise, an annoyed look fills his eyes.

"Who are you?" Eli expresses in a threatening tone, his thick eyebrows furrowing as he stares into what felt like her soul. No matter how gorgeous he is, Sia didn't want to look at him anymore. The girl fell to her knees, slamming to the ground with a thud. Eli closes in on her, kneeling on one knee as his voice grows into a sinister whisper, "You know this means I have to kill you, right?.

CHAPTER 2: PLEASE DON'T KILL ME

Although curiosity can be considered a good trait, it can also get one into trouble.

"No, please! I promise I didn't see anything...o-o-o-or hear anything. Please! let me go. I'm still too young to die! I haven't even made my father proud yet. Please...please...I won't tell anyone. I didn't see anything at all." Sia pleads.

Eli doesn't say anything. It's like a psychological game. He probably wants to see her cry out loud in front of him or maybe he's thinking about the best way to kill her without leaving a trace. After all, there are still people waiting outside, just waiting to come in. Who are those people anyway? Sia has so many questions.

Breaking the silence, Sia, glancing back at the machine, laughs nervously, "It's like you're some kind of alien or something. Heh heh..." No human has the power or technology to make so many people disappear at once. It most definitely felt... extraterrestrial.

Eli raises his brow. "You can call us that. Some people like to call us God, angels, ET... I've heard it all."

"Wa...Wait what, really?" her mind began racing, "Then... then you must have a device that will make me forget everything like... like in that one movie, um, 'Men in Black? 'Can't you use that on me? You can right? You can send me back to my friend! Yeah, send me back to my friend Nadia upstairs! She can send me home and I will forget everything that happened tonight. Can you do that?" Her body is shaking like crazy. Either he kills her now or she'll die from a heart attack very soon.

"No, I've never heard of such a device in my lifetime. But if you came with a friend, I'll probably have to get rid of her too." He sighs in annoyance, scratching his forehead as he thinks about how he can dispose of Nadia's corpse.

"Oh no, oh no, oh no...please don't! Ah, poor Nadia... no. She doesn't know anything I swear. Please don't kill her! This is all just my fault, she had nothing to do with this." Almost accepting her fate, Sia closes her eyes, covering her head with her shaky arms. She shouldn't have brought Nadia into this, it's not her fault.

Eli watches Sia curiously, "Wait, I remember you now. You're the girl who was looking for a restroom earlier." He squints his eyes, "Who are you? A corporate spy? Why are you here anyway?"

"No! No... I'm not. I'm... nobody." She changes her story. She doesn't want to mention anyone. If anyone has to die, it will only be her.

"If you tell me the truth, I can send your body to the right people. In fact, I can promise that your corpse will be intact." Eli speaks in a detached tone.

Too afraid to say it aloud, Sia thinks, "What a jerk!" Who speaks of death this calmly? It was unsettling, to say the least. "I'm willing to die alone. Please... just don't kill anyone else. They don't know anything about you." Sia tries to reason with him, "In fact, Mr. Star, I don't even know why these people are here!"

"Call me Eli. I am not that old...not that it matters of course."

"Fine, Eli. If I am going to die, at least tell me what I'm seeing. What's with all these people and where did those five people disappear to?"

"Those people are waiting for me to send them home. Not only are you delaying my business, but you're also delaying those peoples 'journey back. I'll tell you, but only if you promise to follow me quietly. Just help me send them off as fast as possible too, that would be nice. Make yourself useful before you die and I will be sure to tell you everything before I kill you. How does that sound?" Eli asks. "Also, don't you think about running away because we have cameras everywhere. Don't forget about your friend, too. She's still enjoying the party, yes? Blissfully unaware of the situation you're in. If I cannot find you then I can find her. Do you understand?" Sia can only nod. The girl doesn't really have any other choice. She thinks that maybe if she helps him and does a good job, she may be able to ask for some favors after the job is completed.

Eli asks Sia to help by checking in the names of guests into the system. Actually, not really a name, more like a number, a barcode number. When each person walks into the 'transporter', an elevator-like machine, they scan their wrist on the barcode inside the transporter and Sia must confirm if the face matches with the picture on the screen. This is to make sure Eli doesn't send the wrong person to his planet. Eventually, as time progressed, Sia began to learn more and more information about this night's event.

"These people are sick. We're doing this because they need to go back before it's too late." With his guard lowered, Eli seems less intimidating.

"They don't look sick to me."

"Perhaps to a human but our alien bodies cannot stand the air on earth for too long. Although, I must admit that we are addicted to the smell of the beautiful green leaves and Earth's natural beauty. Alas, it's poison to us, so most of our people can only live on earth for 30 years then they must go back to recuperate." Eli's eyes appeared darker while explaining the suffering of his people.

"Can they come back once they have recovered?" Sia asks, realizing that her job sending off Aliens is almost complete. The last barcodes are scanned and after the push of the magic button, they are gone in an instant.

"Yes, they can but they have to come back with new identities. One day, on our star, is equal to approximately 100 years on earth." Eli pauses, his eyebrows furrowed as if he is in deep thought. "So those humans, who knew them on earth, would be informed only that they died of natural causes."

"Oh... how sad." Sia now understands why his eyes were in sorrow. "So... the party at the dome is actually just a farewell party." Eli nods. "But why did Nadia get an invitation? Oh... oh God...she isn't an alien, is she?" Sia gasps her mouth agape, causing Eli to smile for the first time.

"No, but one of her friends is. It's actually quite beneficial to invite human friends along. We don't want our hotel to look suspicious, we don't need anyone questioning why there are so many cars coming in but no one driving out. Too many rumors and curious inquires are a risk to us."

"So... then what about me?" Sia's voice lowers.

"Yeah... What should I do with this curious young lady?" Eli moves his face closer, staring into her eyes once again. Sia thinks his luminous green eyes remind her of a glowing nebula, striking structure glows brightly in the galaxy.

"I...I won't tell anyone, I promise!" She begs with her hands in prayer, "I will do anything for you. If you need money, I can just ask my dad to send you money! I promise I will be much more useful to you alive than dead!"

"Hmm, but the problem is I don't need money" Eli sighs. "Let's get out of here, I need to think, and I can't do that when I'm hungry."

"Aliens eat too?"

"Of course! How do we get energy if we don't eat? We aren't machines. Actually, even a machine needs an energy source to run." Eli answers before leading her out of the lab. He hasn't mentioned killing her again yet so Sia guesses that she may be safe for now as long as she doesn't say anything unpleasant.

Eli brought Sia back to the masquerade. The guests are all looking at her as they walked in. Who is that girl, walking beside Eli, the Star Hotel's gorgeous President? Sia only hopes Nadia doesn't spot her and Eli or there'll be another missing person to read about in tomorrow's edition. But then she hears someone calling out her name, Sia knows it was too late.

"Hey, Sia! I have been looking all over for you. Where did you go?"

"Nadia! I thought you went back home." Sia wishes that was the case.

"No, not yet. But... um, how?" Nadia whispers to Sia, glancing at Eli.

"It is a long story..." Sia tugs at Nadia's arm, a signal to stop any more embarrassing questions.

"Ah, you must be Nadia, Sia's friend?" Eli introduces himself, inviting Nadia to dinner. Although Sia didn't want Nadia to get involved, it was already too late. At least she won't be alone. Whatever happens, she's just going to go with the flow for now.

.....

"Aliens don't look like what we imagine, Nadia. Your friend is an alien! Believe me, they look just like us!" She screams, "Don't talk to me, Nadia. Go home. Go tell my dad to be careful." Sia's voice is shaking, eyes are closed tightly. "Go home, Nadia! Go now!"

"Sia...Sia...Wake up!" Sia opens her eyes abruptly. "Are you okay? Bad dream?" Worriedly Lisa, her housekeeper, stood over Sia.

"Bad dream?" Sia repeats. "I'm still alive?" She looks around the room slowly. This is her room, she isn't dead yet. Did she really just have a bad dream?

"Where's Nadia?" Sia asks.

"Last night someone dropped you off and left. You were quite intoxicated." Lisa answers. This was not the first time Sia came home drunk.

Sia picks up her phone, dials Nadia's number but there is no answer. It is likely Nadia and her boyfriend are at work. "Was it really a dream?" Sia whispers to herself. She doesn't know who else she should ask other than Nadia. "What if Nadia was killed?" Her imagination runs wild. No, with Nadia being the owner of one of the biggest car dealerships in the state, her disappearance would be huge news. "I'm going to find Nadia," She tells Lisa before getting ready to leave. The only place she may be able to find Nadia is her office but if she isn't there, something isn't right.

"Nadia hasn't come to work yet." Her receptionist informs Sia.

Oh no.

"Thank you." Sia expresses to the receptionist, walking out.

"Is that Nadia's friend?" A salesman asks the receptionist after Sia left the showroom.

"Yeah. Strange, I wonder why she was looking for Nadia."

"Actually, Nadia took a week off. She called in this morning, I thought you knew. Apparently, she got a free ticket to Hawaii so she just took off with her boyfriend. Pretty lucky, eh?" He remarks.

"Ah…" The receptionist lifts her shoulders. "Well…Nadia probably forgot to let Sia know." It is too late to call Sia back, her car had already left the lot. "Hm, oh well, Nadia may contact her later."

"Eli Star…" Whispers Sia, the thought of visiting the alien popping into her head. "No…no…no…What am I thinking? I can't meet him, what if it is true? He'll kill me! No, Sia, don't go back there." Sia ultimately decides to drive back to her house.

For now, it's best to just wait for Nadia's to call or follow the news and see if Nadia's murder gets reported. A horrible thought but at this point, she feels helpless.

.....

Sia hasn't gone outside her home for two days now. There is still no news nor word of Nadia. All Sia had done each day was waiting, sleeping, and watching the news.

"Sia…" Her father calls her. "Come out, now." Lisa informed David that Sia hardly ate a thing in the past 48 hrs and that she is starting to worry about Sia. What if Sia continued to starve herself, Lisa would not know what to do.

Sia opens the door but doesn't say anything, she just stares at her father, waiting to hear him rant and nag her. She is still in her pajamas from last night, her long black hair tied up with a scrunchie.

"Lisa told me you haven't eaten much. Come down, have dinner with me." Her father says, in a worried voice.

"I'm okay, Dad."

"Just come down, I haven't had a chance to see you that much so…" David tries to convince his daughter. He knows she's spoiled but, ever since Sia's mother died from cancer, David always felt guilty for not taking time to notice the symptoms of his wife's disease until it was too late.

"Fine. Give me a couple of minutes. I need to change my clothes." Sia just realizes that she has been in pajamas all day. How time flies.

The dining table is set and ready, Sia comes down from her room. She had a quick shower and put on a new pair of pajamas. Her dad shakes his head in distaste.

"You should go to work with me tomorrow. We have a client who is looking to partner with us and wants to reserve a hotel for his customers from out of state. He said he met you before, actually."

"Who?" Sia asks, not paying much attention. Her mouth is just full of food after unintentionally starving herself for 2 days.

"Eli Star. He is quite well-known among wom…." David hasn't quite completed his sentence, yet, Eli's name already sent shivers down Sia's spine.

" Eli Star? You said Eli Star?"

"Yes, so you know him?" David asks.

"Don't get involved with him, Dad. He is a nightmare! A psychopathic creature!" Sia warns bitterly. Sia doesn't want to tell her dad about her supernatural encounter because at this point, she really isn't sure if whatever she saw that day was real or just a crazy dream. However, one thing she knows for sure is Eli was no dream.

CHAPTER 3: THE SECRET BETWEEN US

Nadia is still missing and the only way Sia can confirm if that night was real is to meet with Eli. Although he scares her, Sia needs to know if and where he's keeping Nadia.

Eli arrives right on time, making her wonder if his 'transporter 'allows him to transport like Doraemon's Magic door.

"Hello, Miss Young. We meet again."

Why would he say 'Miss Young 'when he insists on being called Eli. "Hello, Mr. Star." Sia retorts.

"Please call me, Eli." He smiles sweetly. Sia wanted to call him, "Mr. Nightmare" instead.

"Where's Nadia?" Sia demands angrily after her dad left the meeting room.

"What do you think?" Eli stares at her with the same roguish eyes that he used when he met her in his lab.

"I don't know! I specifically asked you not to do anything to Nadia. She knew nothing and you shouldn't have hurt her. Now, you have the nerve to show up at my father's office. What do you want from me? You better not hurt my dad!" Sia is desperate and fuming. She wished to never see him again but here he is.

"How are you, Sia?" His voice is softer. "I'm glad you are still alive."

"Yeah, thanks to YOU for not killing me yet." Sia says sarcastically. "You're avoiding my question."

"You're welcome." Eli smiles. "If it helps, we're not allowed to kill humans."

"What? But...then... where's Nadia?" Did Eli lie to her the whole time?

"She should be back home by now. Have you tried calling her?" Eli gestures towards her phone.

Sia rings Nadia's phone. Her friend's voice comes through finally.

"Hey Sia. How is it going?" Nadia sounds refreshed.

"Where have you been? I've been worried about you the whole time. Why didn't you pick up the phone?" Sia shouts.

"I got a free trip to Hawaii that night but I had to leave the next day so Robert and I just thought 'what the heck! 'so we just left." Nadia laughs so loud which makes Sia want to spank her friend's butt like a naughty kid for making her so anxious for three days. However, it's also good to know that her friend is safe and sound and that Mr. alien didn't harm her.

"Are you satisfied now, Miss Young?" He teases.

"Don't call me Miss Young."

"I hope you keep to your word and not tell anyone about the other night." Eli's voice is now a bit more serious. This confirms that this whole thing wasn't just a dream. It's real. He is an alien!

"You said you would kill me!" Sia bites her lip, she shouldn't have reminded him.

"I just said we cannot kill humans. Life is precious and we don't really like to kill anyone without good reason." Eli repeats.

"Aren't you afraid I will reveal your secrets?" Her words made Eli laugh.

"Who will believe you?" His eyebrows are furrowed as he looks at her, still smiling. He seems to smile more when he is not at work. "So many alien encounter stories, so much proof, and yet, aliens remain unconfirmed and are mysterious to humans. As for you, who has absolutely no proof, no witness, no photographic evidence whatsoever, people will just think you are a crazy attention seeker."

"How do you know I don't have pictures?" She holds her phone up, wiggling it in his face.

"Electronic devices are automatically disabled upon entering the lab. This is a very basic security system." Eli smirks, Sia rolls her eyes. That explains why she couldn't use her phone that night. Here she was wondering why her battery ran low so fast.

"Then why are you here anyway?"

"You want to know? It's not obvious? I'm working." He answers. "There will be many more Star people coming soon and my hotel is getting overcrowded."

"How about that night you told me you would kill me to keep your secret safe? Were you just lying to me?" Sia snaps.

"You look cute when you're worried. Plus, I just needed to give you a lesson for being nosy." Eli replies casually.

"You..!" Sia clenches her teeth.

"Look, I didn't know who you were until I saw your picture on your father's desk. You think too highly of yourself. I don't have time to track you down for nothing." Eli grins politely before leaving her speechless inside the meeting room.

"I'm an idiot!" Sia really shot herself in the foot this time. What had she done that night before she got back home? The only person who can answer this is her friend, Nadia. She dials Nadia's number once again. "Hey, Nadia. Can I ask you about the last time we hung out? I can't remember what happened."

"That night a few days ago? You just kept drinking until you passed out, weirdo. Eli tried to take your glass away so many times but you kept drinking like the world was going to end. You also kept saying how you were going to die soon" Nadia recalls.

"Who took me back home?"

"Eli drove you and me back home and we dropped you off first. I won a trip to Hawaii that night but I had to leave the next day. It was the criteria for the winner. So Eli recommended that I leave my car at his hotel and he would send someone to pickup Robert and I in the morning. The trip was fantastic!" Nadia smiles. "So we didn't have time to tell anyone."

"Geez...You made me so worried! I thought you were kidnapped or something." Sia sighs softly.

"Who would kidnap me? Eli? If he wants me, he can just snap his fingers and I'll just walk and follow him everywhere." Nadia laughs delightfully. "The only thing I don't understand was how you ran into him that night. Spill the details, girl!" Nadia commands.

Eli was right about one thing, there is no way she can tell anyone about her encounter with an alien. Especially one that looks like a human, a very attractive human. Those aliens don't have big heads and small thin bodies. Besides, they don't fly spaceships like we have imagined. They transmit their bodies via the electromagnetic radiation wavelength aka light. This was Eli's simple explanation of his' transporter'. "We used spaceships a long time ago but that technology became obsolete, and because it attracted too much attention so we stopped using it." He added while telling her the story.

"Well, long story short, I just met him while I went to the restroom and ran into him again when I was looking around at the hallway paintings. We just discussed some of the Native American paintings which you know, I like so...we had something in common I guess. Anyway, he eventually asked me to have dinner at his table. That's all." Sia lies. It was the best way to end the story of her encounter with Eli. From now on, she probably doesn't need to meet him again and everything should be normal. No Eli, no alien, no secret.

.....

Luke has been following Eli's work for a long time but never got a chance to really network with him.With the knowledge of Eli planing to partner with Young Enterprise, he was trying very hard to offer a project to please this client so he can be the one assigned to take care of this prospective partner when the contract is signed.

"Eli has requested that Sia manages the reservations and serves his residents." David hands out a copy of the contract he sent to Young Enterprise for the initial review process. "Finally, Sia will actually do something useful." David beams.

"When did he meet Sia?" Luke is surprised. He had been attending most of the Star partnership meetings and Sia hadn't attended any.

"They did once. I didn't think that Sia could pull it off. I guess I was wrong about her. However, I don't have a problem putting Sia in place to manage this project. Eli also wants her to work at the designated hotel full time taking care of his residents. I think this is a good opportunity for Sia to get her experience managing a hotel too." David says.

Eli requested to reserve one of David's hotels for an entire year and if Young Enterprise can satisfy his guests, Eli would sign an agreement to become a partner with Young Enterprise and provide the funding to either build or remodel a hotel into a permanent resort for his residents. Eli signed long term contacts with those residents so they won't move out and this was done without any heavy ad campaigning. Those are to be his responsibilities. David thinks this is the best project that he has ever had in a long time.

"Dad, what if Sia messes it up. This is a very big project and we shouldn't take a chance. Can we ask him to reconsider his selection for management? I want to take care of this project to make sure things don't go wrong." Luke offers.

"Eli was really pleased with Sia when they met. He actually put her name on the contract to make sure that we assign her as the hotel manager. He must see something in her. So let's give her a chance before we go against Eli's decision. If it happens that Sia does something wrong, we could remind him that he chose her." David insists, this becomes an order to Luke. "From now on, call Sia to attend every Star meeting and when we know which location Eli wants to reserve, then, let HR know to assign Sia as the manager for that site."

Luke is unhappy, but he couldn't do anything now. This was real bad for him, he had worked so hard, hoping to become the leader of the project. He knew from the start that this project was going to be grand. Sia didn't do anything and she just took it out of his hands just like that! Luke clenches his fist.

CHAPTER FOUR: GETTIING CLOSER

Why did Eli request for her to be his new hotel manager? Sia thought he wanted nothing to do with her anymore and she felt the same way. He is her nightmare and the closers she gets to him, the more trouble she will be in.

"I have never asked you to do anything. This is the only thing, Sia." David begs. It was true, her father has never forced her to do anything she didn't want to.

However, this time, her father doesn't know what he is putting himself and her into. He is an alien. An extraterrestrial, from outer space. We, humans, don't know anything about them. Why are so many of them here? What are they planning to do? When will they leave? Nothing. We know nothing about them and now we have to host them like they are special guests.

"Dad, don't you wonder why this deal seems too good to be true. I don't think we should sign the contract, what if this guy's intentions are bad?" Sia worries.

"I don't see anything wrong with the contract," David asserts. "And I don't see anything wrong with you working for him either. We need this project and you have to try your best to work with him. Tomorrow you must go to the hotel site and learn from Elena, the current manager. I already gave Elena a choice to move to another hotel and she is happy about it so she won't give you a hard time or anything."

"Dad!" Sia shouts.

"If you don't do a good job this time, don't you ever call me Dad again. Sia, this time I really mean it." David contends.

This time, Sia realizes that she really has no choice. She has to work with an alien. A very crafty one at that. Previously at the office he said he had no intention to bother her but now he specifically put her name on the contract to serve him. What does he want from her exactly?

.....

A week of training has gone by aimed at getting Sia ready to manage Eli's designated hotel. Eli picked the one near the Airport as he mentioned to her before that his people were required to travel often. That was also one of the reasons why the aliens decided to stay in the U.S.

"Americans and Europeans are like fishes and birds. They can go anywhere in the world as long as there is a river or a sky. So holding an American or European passport is the best choice for us." Eli told her.

"How do you even obtain a U.S. passport if you are not a U.S. citizen?" Sia wondered.

"That is one of my jobs here..." Eli answered but didn't go into the details. However, Sia can guess. Making a fake identity is not new after all. With his power and connections, those things are not hard to do.

"Sia..." a familiar voice calls from behind.

"Oh...man," Sia whispers to herself. "I'm thinking about the supernatural and here comes a devil!"

"Why are you here?" Eli pretends. His obvious fake shocked expression makes Sia want to slap him really hard.

"You know why I HAVE to be here, Mr. Star." Sia answers.

"Eli. Call me Eli, please. Or you can call me boss. I mean, I am your boss again." He smiles. His face, when he smiles, is nice but Sia hates his smile so much because every time he smiles, its like he is mocking her.

"Why are you here anyway?" Sia changes the topic, making herself appear a little more professional.

"I hired an architect to plan some additional construction and decorate my office." Replies Eli.

"Your office? What about the downtown one?" Sia questions. Why does he want to have an office here?

"Since you were able to infiltrate that secure site, it's not considered a safe workplace anymore." He mutters sarcastically and accuses her at the same time.

"Are you for real?" Sia doesn't like it when she cannot believe half of his words. "Can you be a little bit more serious when you talk with me please?"

"I am serious." Eli laughs. "Damn serious! Do you know why I put you to work at this site?"

"Because I know your secrets." Sia exclaims rather quickly.

"Smart girl! I have been looking to expand our housing for a long time but I have no resources and no people here. You came at the right time. I know you aren't happy with the contract but I really do need your help." His voice is more convincing this time.

Now Sia feels very guilty. After all, he isn't trying to bully her but he seems to have good intentions to work with her on helping his residents.

"Do I unintentionally misunderstand him?" Sia questions herself. Even though she snuck into his private office, he forgave her. Then he gave her food and drinks and sent her home safely. He even helped her dad with a new business opportunity. All she did was cause him trouble and complain about him. Sia shuts her eyes and takes a deep breath.

"Be more professional, Sia. Be more professional..." She warns herself. "Do you want me to show you around?"

"That would be nice, thank you!" He smiles again, this time a little more sincere.

"Will you bring more 'people 'here to earth?" Sia begins her investigation.

"Yes."

"Why do you bring so many anyway?" Sia voices concern. "Are you trying to start a war or something?"

"Apparently, watching too many Hollywood movies is bad for you." He replies. "We have been here on earth for the longest time. If we wanted to start a war, we would've settled such a conflict long ago."

"Then why? Why are so many of your people here?"

"Don't forget, we live a shorter life on earth. There is no point for us to start a war with humans when we can only live here for 30 years. Just think about it. If you have only 30 years to live, what would you like to do?" This is always Eli's style of answering a serious question. He answers a question with another question. This means he basically doesn't want to answer her at all.

"How many aliens are on earth?" Despite him not truly answering her questions, Sia is still going to try to get the most information she could.

"Many. We are among humans all over the world. I only know the number here in New Mexico. There are many more elsewhere." Eli glances at his watch and teased, "I think I need to charge you for each question now."

"Fine, last one...for now...please?" Sia lifts a single finger. Eli doesn't say no so Sia just shoots another one. "How do you differentiate alien from human?"

"Did you know I was an alien when you first saw me?"

"No." Sia shakes her head.

"Then you wouldn't know who is. But most aliens are very attractive when you get to know them. This is a special character that we, aliens, have developed over time. Otherwise, we could not live with humans this long. Attractive doesn't only mean a good appearance but it can be more intelligent, kinder, more charismatic, more creative. The more we can make humans adore us, the safer we will be." He turns his face and looks at her with his deep beautiful green eyes again. Now Sia knows why she felt that he intentionally flirted with her that night. It was his protection mechanism. "Don't fall for it, Sia. Don't fall for it!" She tells herself.

"Have you ever fallen in love with a human?" Sia continues her question.

"Sorry, this little Q&A has already ended with your previous question. Another question will cost you something you don't want to lose." He raises his eyebrows and smiles.

Sia quickly turns around. She knows her face is blushing because she feels suddenly hot. Sometimes, she just doesn't understand why she wants to keep talking to him, even though she doesn't really trust his words.

"Already lunchtime? Perhaps you can take me someplace nice to eat?" Eli suggests.

Maybe if she goes out with him, he will answer more questions.

"Alright," She nods before leading him to an elevator which is used only by the employees, separate from the guest elevator.

"We have a small canteen down in the basement. Our food is cooked by our top chef so it's pretty good. Now will be a good chance for you to try." Sia brags, pressing a button to the 'B 'level.

Just as the pair is about to reach their destination, the elevator suddenly stops. Sia feels a little bit embarrassed because this machine malfunction should not have happened in this fairly new facility. She keeps pressing the 'B 'button over and over until she hears a loud snap. Suddenly, the elevator begins to fall so fast that it makes Sia dizzy, causing her to fall down onto the floor, screaming. The elevator line is running loose and it keeps falling lower and lower to the ground. The lights cut out, Sia just realizes this is a very dangerous situation but there is nothing more she could do other than scream. Eli instinctively pulls Sia close to his chest. He uses both arms to shield her before the box crashes to the floor, his head hitting the ground, knocking him out right away.

Sia is safe but the room is in complete darkness. Unable to see she moves her hands around and all she can feel is a thick liquid from Eli's head. "Eli!" Sia cries before the elevator doors are pulled open.

"Call 911. We need an ambulance." One of the employees shouts to a security guard.

"Are you okay, Miss Young?" The maintenance man asks.

"I am okay but look! Eli's hurt, he's bleeding. Help him!" Sia screams. Her hands are covered in blood, and unsure if she's injured. She doesn't feel any pain, maybe it is adrenaline, but she is sure it was nothing. It all happened so fast but Sia remembers Eli holding her very tight to save her. She wished she could have helped him more but all she can do now is to apply pressure to his wound, to slow the bleeding. An alien can bleed...

Sia and Eli are being transported to the emergency room. Doctors order multiple diagnostic tests and scans. The results come back, Eli only sustained lacerations to the scalp and his back. Sutures are placed in the ER room for Eli and he is observed by the ER nurse until Eli wakes up two hours later, holding his head in pain.

The traumatic wound itself is not as bad as the effect of human medication. It makes his head spin like crazy. Eli closes his eyes tight, with teeth clenched together.

"Argh," He cries out finally.

"Eli…" Sia calls his name. "Are you okay?" Out of guilt, she feels he was not really her nightmare but she is his. Since she met him, he is always in trouble.

"I'm- I am okay…" Eli answers as he tries to get out of the bed as quickly as he can. His pain is obvious from his expression Sia gently lays him back onto the bed. "Don't go, you're hurt. Do you remember what happened?" She asks the same questions the doctor has asked her earlier.

"I cannot stay here for too long. I have to go. Sia, tell them that I am okay now and I need to be discharged." He's begging her, his eyes anxious and sorrowful. Sia takes the hint, nodding before rushing to the counter.

The nurse comes back with Sia and asks Eli the same questions Sia has asked just a few minutes ago. Eli tries to smile for the nurse to show that he is fine and ready to be discharged. She checks his wound and finally agrees that he can leave after all of Sia's persuading.

"The sutures look great. After I remove your IV, you should be able to go soon." The nurse ensured and left the room.

"Are you sure, you're okay?" Sia asks Eli again.

"We heal faster than humans. If I am here for too long, they'll get suspicious. I need to leave now, I am okay, don't worry." Eli whispers. Yet another secret she feels an obligation to keep.

Sia drives him back to his Downtown office, he doesn't want anyone else to see him. Within a day, all his wounds are completely healed. The word "heal" for an alien simply means that his skin has completely regenerated as though he was never injured. No blood, no scars.

"Do you feel pain like humans?" Sia wonders.

"We can feel pain but once the wounds heal the pain subsides completely." He answers. Now Sia understands why he used his body to protect her, he knew he wouldn't die from the injury.

"Do you know what happened to the elevator?" He noticed the same thing as Sia that the hotel elevator malfunction was suspicious.

"I haven't had a chance to investigate but I am planning to do that tomorrow. All I know from maintenance is that the lines were torn which caused the elevator to fall. Luckily no one else was hurt other than you."

CHAPTER 5: WHO'S THE TARGET

Sia and Eli guessed it right, the elevator lines were cut. Were they the intended victims? Did someone plan this catastrophe for her, for Eli, or both?

"Who do you think was suppose to be the target?" The question causes Sia to jump out of the chair before shaking her arms to get rid of the weird feeling that she is now experiencing.

"Do you have any enemies?" Sia looks at Eli.

"I have one. About 2 weeks ago, she came to my lab and I caught her." Eli answers casually. Sia was astounded by his replay, she wishes he could take things a bit more serious when he talked to her now that they were in a professional relationship as boss and subordinate. "No one knew I was coming here today so the target is definitely not me." Eli exclaims. "This incident was planned ahead and the killer knew you would be working. We aren't booking any hotel rooms at this time so there are no clients, only employees and construction workers. Unless this was just an extremely unlucky day, you ARE the target." Presumes Eli.

"What? NO!" Sia shakes her head. "No way. It is not me. No!" Sia has never harmed anyone. All she has ever done before working here was spend money and have fun. She did argue with her father from time to time but to think that her dad wanted to kill her is preposterous!

"Let's not worry about it yet. Maybe it was really just an accident. The best thing you can do is to report the incident to the police and just wait and see. In the meantime, I'll go to work at the airport site every day, we can gather more information. If you stay close to me, I will not let anyone harm you." Eli assures her in a calmer voice. Eli's voice is normal again as is his wound. He asks Sia to remove the sutures from his back. Sia removes the sutures and watches as out of place. His ruptured skin automatically closes itself. Sia looks at him, amazed with his super healing ability.

"Thank you for today." Sia finally says, Eli smiling in return.

"I thought I would never hear you say that." He teases.

"So, when are your people coming?" Sia worries that the broken elevator may cause the construction to be delayed.

"Everything has to be completed by next week. Otherwise, I have to leave here to report the delays on my planet which means I have to leave earth for more than a year which is not practical for me to do." Eli explains.

"I will make arrangements with my dad to source more contractors to help out. We may have to recruit from out of state. The costs will be higher but that is the only way to keep construction on time." Sia sounds like a businesswoman, she realizes that her life has changed a lot since she met him.

"We don't have a problem with money. So if you need help, let me know. For us, time is much more valuable."

"I understand." Sia nods.

David is not happy about hiring more people to fix the problem but it was on the contract and he was obligated to honor it. The only news that consoled her father down was that Eli and She were not hurt badly in the accident. Otherwise, things could've gotten a lot uglier.

However, Sia had not told her father about their suspicion that the elevator accident was not an ordinary accident but may have been planned. She doesn't want him to worry about her too much. This was the first time that her dad ever trusted her to work alone without Luke's supervision. That was the reason why she didn't like to work for her dad before. Luke had taken all the credits for her hard earned work. The Star project is a little different. Eli specifically asked to limit the employees' involvement from the Young enterprise except for Sia. Of course, Sia knew why Eli made that a condition for accepting a contract with Young Enterprise. Every single resident at the hotel is an alien and keeping human involvement to a minimum guaranteed the secrecy of star project.

The additional contractors begun to slowly arrive and the work has been progressing smoothly for the last 3 days when Sia received an unsettling letter from the labor union about the workers' complaint of unfair wages. The letter demanded an equal wage for all workers. The local workers complained that the out of town contractors were getting more pay than the local union workers.

"We haven't had a raise for years and now new employees are getting paid more than us." The union leader stated. It is true the hotel employees haven't received a raise for the past two years because the tourism industry was staggering but compared to other hotels, their employee salary is not low at all. Besides, each year every employee receives a bonus to subsidize the raises during tough times and no one had ever complained about it. Why now? Sia feels like it was her karma because of all the things she did to her father. There were union signs up in front of the hotel and the employees are demonstrating their disapproval.

While David negotiates with the union leader, Sia tries to calm the workers down in her father's office. Eli rushes to the hotel after receiving word from Sia that morning.

"How is everything? Are you okay?" He sounds worried.

"I asked the out of town contractors to work on your office for now. The elevator was fixed but someone vandalized the structure and some building materials were stolen last night, we have to reorder what was stolen." Sia reports.

"That's okay. Just make sure to finish the interior including the guest rooms on time. That will be fine." Eli briefs.

"I am so sorry about all this, Eli. This shouldn't have happened. We have always been on good terms with our employees and we have never had this sort of problem before." Sia explains.

"What do they want?" Eli asks.

"They want a raise but the amount is unreasonable. If we give them more, then we have to do the same for the rest of our labor force. As you know, business is not stable and we just signed with you so there is no way we can meet their demands." Sia shakes her head while the crowd outside her office gets louder.

"Be careful, do not confront them." Eli glances at the protesters, noticing one man who seems to be more aggressive than the others. "Who is that man? I have never seen him before." Eli asks.

"His name is Anthony, one of the maintenance workers. He works mostly at the main building where our central office is located." Sia answers.

"Then why is he here?" Eli wonders.

"Not sure. Maybe he's part of the union... no clue other than that. But I have met him once, he seems to be leading the strike but he is not a coordinator because the union committee is meeting with my dad right now." Sia remarks.

"I'll go out and talk with them for a bit."

"'I'll come with you." Eli squints his eyes but Sia insists, "I know most of them well. I'll be okay, besides, you'll be with me anyway..." She forces a smile.

Eli nods but before he leaves the room, he requests for a security team to provide them some backup. Next, he starts by introducing himself and announces his plan for developing this hotel for future residents. "I have always been supportive of fair wages and I will continue to support that. However, I cannot do that if our hotel is still under construction. That is why we had to hire another contractor, to help us reach our goal and open on time. Right now, Mr. Young is in a meeting with the union, and I hear he is also trying his best to get our work schedule back on track and to assure every employee is happy." Eli announces calmly.

Everyone is listening to him and some are even nodding their head in agreement until Anthony shouts, "But we want the answer now! We need a raise. You need to promise us a raise right NOW. Otherwise, we will bring construction to a halt" He demands while pushing the crowd of protesters. A scream breaks from the crowd and a body is thrown causing picket signs to crash down, Eli blocks Sia from the flying debris with his shoulder.

"Are you okay?" Sia realizes that now her body is underneath Eli and the crowd is throwing signs at him. The protestors continue to scream, as police and security guards start to disperse the loud and rowdy assembly.

"Go inside!" Eli warns Sia, opening the office door for her. He looks upset. It was a look that she had never seen before. Not long after they went back inside, Eli's personal guard comes in.

"Sia, this is Jace. He helps me with research and personal matters. Can he work here during the construction?" Eli didn't need to ask. After all he's the boss.

"Of course." Sia answers.

Eli's instinct tells him that something is not right about this labor strike. Jace helps him with the illegalities and legalities of the alien business. When Eli leaves earth, Jace manages his hotel and "transporter'" and it has been this way since Eli started his hotel business. To say the least he trusts Jace.

"Can you investigate him for me?" Eli points to Anthony who is still shouting among the protesters outside. He provides Jace with known details and incidents about Anthony. Jace takes Anthony's picture and calls a connected source.

Jace is a big man with very short hair whose skin is a bit darker than Eli's. He doesn't talk much but Eli told Sia that Jace relies on telepathy a lot and that he is good at it. Aliens can only telepathically communicate with other aliens but Eli thinks Jace might even be able to read human minds as well.

"I've never seen him before." Sia wonders.

"He just came. He normally comes two or three days before the new visitors arrive to help me with paperwork. He doesn't have plans to stay long on earth unless he has to replace me when it comes time for me to go home. Eli explains.

Sia's cell phone rings. Her dad had adjourned the meeting with the union and the executive board had offered a temporary raise to the local contractors but the union had not agreed yet. At least not until they have talked to a protesters. In the meantime, the mob agreed to go home.

Eli posts a job-listing for contractors looking to pick up some overtime that pays twice the hourly rate. He also hires more security guards to watch over the workers and hotel property during the night shift.

Early the next day, Sia notices Eli and Jace have already arrived at her office.

"Did you go home last night?" She surprisingly asks.

"I did, and we've only been here long enough to close the door. Sia, I have a question for you. Who is Luke Young?" Jace put together a profile on Anthony last night. But Eli recalled hearing Luke's name at a previous meeting but he didn't really pay much attention to him then. However, his name popped up again but this time as a Young.

"He is my adopted brother. Why?" Sia wonders. Hasn't she mentioned Luke? Does she not like him enough to avoid uttering his name.

"Is Anthony working for Luke? Recently, a large sum of money was transferred to his account from Luke's secretary, Beth." Eli queries. He got a print out of Anthony's bank statement.

Sia raises her eyebrows. "How did you get that?"

"Jace can do many things that others cannot," Eli explains, complimenting Jace.

"I heard Beth and Anthony are a couple but I am not really sure. It may also just be a rumor too. Luke has many people working for him. He is like my father's right hand. He has been working for my father for a long time. Long before me. My dad even threatened that he would give his company to him every time we argued. That is how much he loves him." Sia exclaims with anger.

Slowly Eli starts to understand the situation. He believes Sia is dealing with Luke's jealousy. Luke is definitely completing with her for David's attention because she is the only biological child.

"Luke cannot justify his power in the company if you and your father have a good work relationship, because he preys on your ill relationship with David. Luke's seniority grows stronger every time you fumble" Eli concludes. "Sia, I think the elevator trap was meant for you. I believe you are the intended target."

"No way!" Sia shouts. "I don't like him and I don't think he likes me that much but we have known each other for a long time. I don't think…"Sia stops to rethink Eli's theory. But if the elevator incident was successful, Luke would benefit the most from a failed project. He would benefit by replacing her.

"Jace left to converse with Anthony and to gather any intel of any planned protests on the property." Eli informs Sia. His eyes are cold.

Even though Eli claims aliens can't kill humans, Sia still hopes nothing bad befalls to Anthony.

CHAPTER 6: I'M YOUR DOOMED FATE

The meeting between the union leader and the construction workers went smoothly yesterday. Sia didn't see Anthony at the meeting, not even a glimpse of his shadow. The executive board approved a temporary pay raise for the construction workers in exchange for their agreement to return to work ASAP to complete the construction on time.

Sia finally scheduled an appointment with an interior designer to come out today, so she can start purchasing office furnitures. Eli had seemed pleased with the building design, especially his office. Sia had the architect put in a glass curtain wall similar to Eli's downtown office because Sia knew Eli loved to look at the mountains. Sia also added a sofa bed for Eli's office because he often worked late into the evening. This way, if he gets too tired he'll have a place to lay down and rest. Sia asked Eli if he wanted to have a room reserved for him to rest on days he worked late but he had refused. Eli preferred to go home every day no matter how late he worked.

Lynn, Sia's secretary, made unsubstantiated assumptions that Eli must have a girlfriend who waits for him at home which is why he had to go home every day. Sia pinched her for saying that but at the same time, she wondered the same thing. After all, no one knows where Eli lives and no one dares to ask him.

"Sia, do you have time today? I need to visit the adopted families, just come with me." Eli steers Sia away from her desk and whispers in her ear. She found this sudden closeness uncomfortable and wondered if he was aware of rules that prohibited workplace harassment and intimidation, especially those that may be constructed as sexual in nature. As much as she felt he threatened her personal space, she did not have the heart to report him. At least he has never asked her to go to bed with him or anything like that yet.

"Wait, Eli! I'm still working." Sia complains.

"Yes, I know. You are working for me that is why I asked you to come with me." Eli retorts.

"No, what I meant was...ah...never mind" Sia decides to let it go. "May I grab my purse first before we leave?"

"Yes, of course." He smiles suddenly being less pushy.

Sia walks back to her desk and turns off her computer. Lynn gives her boss a foxy look. "Good luck!" She smiles teasingly to Sia.

"Where are we going?" Sia asks after having driven like 30 minutes without Eli saying a word. She is not familiar with the road they traveling on.

"There is a Native American tribe that we believed to have descended from our Star planet because they all have telepathic abilities. That's how we communicate with them. They are like us. Although they do not identify themselves as of any star planet aliens. However, they have been helping us raise our little Star people, as young as 15 years of age for many generations now. Yesterday Jace told them about you. Now they want to meet you.

"Meet me? Why?" Sia opens her mouth, a surprised gesture.

"Maybe to get to know you. We shall find out today." Eli answers.

"Have you met them before?"

"I met their ancestors. Many of them are still on the Star planet." Eli pauses for a while before continuing the story. "We have a strict rule over there. They cannot announce that they are of alien descent nor show their alien abilities. If anyone breaks the rule, the person is sent back to the Star planet and some have been sent back before."

"That's sad." Sia exhales morosely.

"But if the Star people did not have that rule, potential harm to them by humans is inevitably very great. The reason this tribe helps us is to ask us for forgiveness for them breaking the rule so we agreed to their request. Some of the kids arriving on earth in their care are actually the children of people sent back to Star Planet.

After a four hour drive and another hour hiking on foot, Eli and Sia finally arrive at a small Native American village hidden deep in the mountain. The village is small with few houses and one big adobe lodge. Children are playing everywhere, and none of them are carrying electronic devices like the children in urbanized areas.

Eli leads Sia into the big adobe house. The interior of the house resembled an institutionalized facility like a school. It's a two-story house made of red mud and big logs. A young lady walks out to greet them and introduces herself as Yana. She has long dark hair and is very tall for a woman.

"Is she a Star person?" Sia whispers to Eli and he nods. "They all are."

Yana takes us to meet a middle-aged man named Carl. Carl is blind but he walks and moves around like he can see. If you do not see that his eyes are closed, you would think they were wide open.

The first impression that Sia gets when entering Carl's room is that Carl is a herbalist because she smelled dry flowers and herbs. They makes her sneeze right away. Eli holds her shoulder and smiles at her.

"Carl is a medicine man. He teaches herbal medicine to the kids here. He is also the leader of the community." Eli tells Sia. Sia is not far off in her intuition after all.

"Thank you for coming." Carl said. "Yana, how about you take them to get a drink of water. You must have traveled a long way. There are no grocery stores around here." Yana nods and takes us to a table outside the lodge before bringing us two glasses of water. "Carl will come out soon. He just finished teaching a class before you arrived."

"Not a problem. We can wait." Eli says and Yana walks back inside the house.

"Is Carl also from the Star planet?" Sia asks.

"He was born on earth, he is one of the Natives. His tribe doesn't have too many members left. In fact, he might be the only original member in this village. Others including Yana were sent here to be near us. Yana has been here for 20 years. She teaches and takes care of the children for Carl. There is also Mia but I haven't seen her. She is usually the person who contacts us if they need anything for the kids such as food, money, toys, books and so forth. I don't mean to sound like they are financially dependent on us. The people in this village are very self-sustaining. They grow their own food and raise their own animals. They hardly ask us for anything." Eli explains. "Oh...by the way, I already informed your father that this will be an overnight business trip."

"What?" Sia opens her mouth. "I can't. I didn't bring a tooth brush or extra clothes to wear.

"Lisa packed a bag for you. It is in the trunk of the car." Eli drinks his glass of water and avoids eye contact with Sia.

"Eli, you..." Sia stammers, "Why did you do that? You should have asked me first before you finalized these arrangements."

"I asked your father for his permission to let you stay here overnight and he said, yes." He argues, sipping his cup. Sia rolls her eyes and sighs. His controlling behavior is getting on her nerves and there was nothing she could do about it. Sia feels defeated.

"Thank you very much for coming." Carl finally comes out. Eli stands up and gestures to the seat next to Sia. "So I hear you aren't one of the Star people." Carl turns his face toward her.

"Yes. My involvement with the Star people was by accident. Eli said you are a descendent of the Star people." Sia inquires.

"It is a long story but now it is only me. Everyone is gone now. My wife passed more than 5 years ago. She was also human and I honestly thought I would die before her but it turns out she left me first." Carl smiles when mentioning his wife. Sia guesses he must be sad but people do heal from loss, eventually with time.

"Eli said you wanted to see me about something." Sia states becoming curious.

"Ah yes. If you don't mind, may I borrow your hand?" Carl opens his hand out to Sia.

Sia looks at Eli. He nods so she put her hand in his.

"Can I have yours too?" Carl asks Eli and Eli gives his hand to Carl.

While holding their hands, Carl begins praying or chanting. Sia suddenly feels light-headed and somewhat dizzy. A luminous shining light enters her mind then she notices someone there, someone is sitting next to a big tree.

"Who are you?" Sia steps closer for a better look. She recognizes the person. It is Eli. His face is pale and contorted like he is in a lot of pain. He coughs into his hands. Both hands are instantly covered in blood.

Eli pulls his hand back from Carl. His eyes look dreadful. "Excuse me for a second." Eli stands up quickly and walks away.

Sia wasn't really sure what had happened. Was that a future vision she just saw? She asks herself but Carl answers. "If you are together, that will be his ending."

Now Sia understands why Eli was spooked off.

Eli hasn't said anything since they have left the village and Sia also knows not to bother him with the vision she just saw. Eli drives to a near by town and parks in front of a small hotel. He books two rooms and gives one key to her. He helps carry her bag and sets it in front of her room. He looks tired and worn out. Sia doesn't know if it was a good idea meeting Carl. Carl's special ability is that he can foresee the future and it appears that he asked to see her because he had some premonition that Eli and Sia may become intimately involved. Carl wanted to warn Eli of the consequences of involving himself with Sia. That is his doomed fate.

Sia was also in shock. Although the vision in her mind was blurred, the dying man was most definitely Eli. What Sia doesn't understand is that she thought aliens couldn't die. At least that was what Eli had her believe from the start.

.....

Sia hasn't seen Eli since the trip. The hotel construction and the interior design for his office was completed a day early. She wanted to tell him but he was nowhere to be found.

Yesterday Jace arrived with the residents and she checked them in and there is still no sign of Eli. Jace told her in advance that Eli would be at the Downtown office until all the guests had arrived safely. Sia wanted to offer to help him but she also had her hands full here at the Airport hotel. She was new to hotel management but still she stress-tested her staff before the reopening so things would go smoothly.

Despite the check-in part, Sia did a pretty good job settling all of her new residents at the hotel. Later on David called and gave her a nice compliment. The Airport hotel was lively again after being vacant during the renovation project. The only thing Sia was hoping for right now is for her alien boss to come and see his new office.

Eli transferred payment to the airport hotel for the residents. The hotel was completely booked for a full year. David and the board members are extremely happy with the outcome. Sia finally got an invitation to attend the board member meeting at the main office. They congratulated her and asked if Sia knew of anything else that may make Eli happy. Sia doesn't even know if Eli is happy with her right now. She hadn't seen him for weeks.

It was strange without Eli. He was so annoying and always caused her to run- around without advance appointment. All the business meals, meeting clients away from the city, exploring and searching for Indian artifacts like pottery and paintings, and jogging 5 miles at the park. But when he is not here, she felt like she has no purpose.

The board meeting has finally ended. Sia hardly understood or heard what they were saying.

"You need to attend more meetings, Sia. After all, you are my daughter." David pats her on the back.

"You are so lucky, Mr. Young. You have two good kids." Several committee members compliment David after the meeting.

"Thank you. Sia is still new. I hope she learns more from everyone." David replies looking humbled.

"Hello, Miss Young." Sia heard a man's voice from behind. "We have never been officially introduced."

"Oh...Sia." Her dad interrupts. "This is Anderson Miller. He is the director of our Public Relations department. This is my daughter, Sia. She just graduated. She does not have much experience managing a business yet, and will need your help a lot. I am sure you will understand each other being that you are both from the same generation."

"Can I call you Sia?" Anderson asks.

"Yes, please." Sia nods. She noticed throughout the meeting that he was staring at her the whole time. It actually made her a little bit uncomfortable.

"I leave you to talk with each other. I have to go. See you later Anderson." David waves and leaves.

"I was going to see you at your hotel to make a Press Release on our Airport hotel contract with Mr. Star. Luckily, you are here today. Do you have time for a quick chat?" Anderson asks.

"Yes. But I don't have an office here. Do you want to visit our office at the Airport later when you have free time? Sia offers.

"I am free now. How about we just go today?" Anderson enthusiastically replies. Since Sia doesn't have any plans elsewhere she agrees to it.

"I have never seen Mr. Star. I heard he is quite charming." Anderson mentions, taking multiple photos of the hotel building. "We need some pictures for our Press Release."

"Please do not photograph our guests. They are quite concerned about their privacy. Eli is the same. He rarely allows anyone to take his photo." Sia warns.

"You seem close to him." Anderson muses.

"He is my boss so I have to learn things that he likes and doesn't like." Sia answers before Anderson makes anymore wild guesses that may not hold true.

Anderson collects information as he interviews her. Lynn comments on why Anderson has to come and interview Sia in person. "He could have just asked his PR assistant to come and do it. I think he came because of you, Sia." Lynn whispers.

"It's just for work, it doesn't matter who conducts the interview." Sia scolds her assistance.

However, it turns out that Lynn was not wrong. Anderson came back again the next day asking her to continue their meeting over lunch. Sia doesn't want to go but he keeps on begging. "I want to treat you for helping me yesterday."

"It is my job anyway. Please don't worry." Sia replies with an expression of disinterest.

"You seem worried about going out with me. Is your boss keeping you from other men?" Anderson teases. Sia rolls her eyes and finally agrees to go with him just to stop him from bothering her.

"Only today, okay? I prefer to have lunch with my co-workers because we have many projects that have to get done by the end of this week." Sia lies.

"It won't take very long I promise." Anderson smiles and points her to his car which is parked in front of the hotel.

Anderson brought some photos and a draft of the Press Release to get an approval from her.

"Wow... that's fast!" Sia exclaims.

"We hope to get Eli's photos to go with the letter. Do you have some at the office?" Anderson asks.

"It is not going to be possible unless he gives you permission to take it. I don't know of any press that has been successful in getting one." Sia states.

It would be interesting to see Anderson asking Eli to consent to a photo session. Sia thinks.

CHAPTER 7: DON'T YOU DARE TOUCH MY WOMAN

Eli buried himself with work as soon as he returned from Chaco Canyon with Sia. Working is the only way to keep him busy so he can forget the vision he saw and to keep his distance from Sia. He knew all along what was going to happen to him if he got close to Sia but Eli believes this isn't the first time he had met her.

"Sia looked like Anna but she was not Anna, she can't be." Jace reminds him. Eli met Anna nearly 300 years ago in Scotland. Both look exactly the same except their hair color. "You've been on Earth for way too long and it's only natural that you're going to find someone that looks the same. You should know that." Jace looks at his poor friend knowing quite well how he feels. Jace knows both Sia and Anna and he still doesn't understand how two women can look and act like the same person.

"I left her once and I don't know if I can leave her again." Eli confesses. His eyes show a painful state of emotion, reflecting on his past.

"Let her go. Aliens and humans can never be together anyway. We aren't vampires that can immortalize her with a single bite." If vampires really existed, their love lives would definitely be easier than aliens Jace reflected. "By the way, I have some news for you. Is it good or bad? You can decide that for yourself." He shows his phone to Eli.

"Sia Young, heiress of Young enterprise on a date with Anderson Miller, the Young enterprise executive board director and the owner of a popular web marketing platform. Both single with approval from the Young family…" Without even reading the entire article, Eli's face turns red. Jace rushes to get his phone back before Eli decides to throw it out of the window.

"Who is that guy?" Eli demands, his voice becoming stern and callous.

"I'm showing this to you because I was hoping that you would let them be. I mean they look like a nice couple. That way you don't have to worry about her anymore." Jace puts his phone in his pocket while patting his friend's shoulder. Eli brushes Jace's hand away.

"I thought you said you were going to get your car serviced." Eli changes the topic. "You should go now. I have work to do." Eli doesn't really feel like talking anymore. Sia said Jace doesn't talk much but Eli thinks he talks all the time, he especially likes to annoy Eli with things he doesn't want to hear.

"Hey…I know what you are thinking, Eli. You have an ill fate with her. You better not start again."

Eli takes a deep breath, counting numbers in his mind. He knows Jace can read minds and Jace should know that he is about to be kicked out of the room very soon if he doesn't leave Eli alone.

.....

"What do you mean 'married 'dad? I don't want to marry anyone, especially him. I've only know him like 3 days and met him twice." Sia shouts when her father tells her to consider marrying Anderson.

"I don't think he's bad. He is a businessman with a well-known family business in Denver. He is also a shareholder in our company." David tries to convince his daughter.

"His family owns dispensaries and his money in our company is probably from drugs alone. Dad...please. I don't know him and I don't like him. Please have that report taken down from the web, otherwise, I'm going to sue them. The news is absolutely fake." Sia's sure that the person who leaked the news was probably Anderson too. She was not some type of a popular celebrity so why is there a picture of him and her on some sleazy internet gossip column.

"You are nearly 25 years old. You won't stay young forever, Sia. I want to hold grandchildren before I die." Her father is at his old tricks\ again.

"Dad, you will live until you are 100 years old. Don't worry about holding any grandkids yet. Now I've just started working and I'm trying to stay on track for my career. I don't want to get involved with love or any distractions. Please...Dad. Tell Anderson that he shouldn't bother me and just worry about doing his job." Sia insists and walks out of the dinning room.

Her cell phone begins to ring at just the right time. Of course Nadia received the news and started bombarding her with questions too. "It's fake news I swear! Just drop it, please. People have been asking me all day." Sia shouts at the phone.

"Alright, whatever. Anyway, I'm at Izzy, you want to hang?" Nadia asks, referring to 'Izzy,' a local karaoke bar. Sia hasn't been there for a while so she decides it may be a good idea to just drop by and release some tension with a couple of songs tonight.

"Sure, I'll meet you there." Sia agrees and runs up the stairs to change her clothes before grabbing her car keys.

The only good thing about going to pubs here is that there are no lines. New Mexico is just a quiet state with small cities unlike New York or Las Vegas where you have to wait in line to get in. Besides, the staff here know Sia and Nadia well. They are the usuals here after all. Although she hasn't had any time since she started working with Eli, her usual seats are still available upon request.

"Hey! Sia! How are you? Long time no see, girl." Nadia waves with both hands in an excited motion.

"Good, good. How's Robert?" Sia doesn't know why Nadia hasn't married her boyfriend yet. They have been together since high school.

"He's good. Busy as usual." She shrugs, "What about you and Eli? Y'all are working together now right?" Nadia's voice becomes higher in pitch, a shine in her eyes as she talks about Eli.

"Yeah, he's my boss but I hardly see him." Sia bit her lip trying not to spill any sensitive information about him. It's tempting to fill in the gaps for a friend when one knows a celebrity but she can't do that to Eli.

"Ah...so he is still a mystery man huh?"

Sia just grins.

"How about that guy on the news? What's his name?" Nadia asks.

"Ah! Sia, is that you?" Speak of the devil! Anderson walks in with two glasses of Margaritas, a New Mexican favorite. Nadia covers her mouth with both hands as Sia turns around in surprise, almost falling out of her chair.

"What a coincidence to meet you here, eh?" Anderson turns to Nadia, "Lemme guess, you're Sia's friend?"

"Yes, Nadia." She answers quickly.

"Anderson. Nice to meet you." He introduces himself, holding out his hand which Nadia shakes hesitantly.

"Yeah no. Mr. Miller, sir, I don't believe in coincidences. Please just leave us alone. I don't want to share any more headlines with you, thank you." Sia stares at him in disgust.

"Look, I would like to offer my apologies. I really don't know how that news came out." He defends himself, rubbing his neck. Sia continues staring at him." Fine, at least let me explain." Anderson begs.

"Nadia, I think the night is spoiled. Let's call it a day and go home." She stands up and grabs her purse.

"Wait, but Sia! we just got here." Nadia whines, her eyebrows scrunches in confusion.

"Sia, please be reasonable, your friend is here. Nobody will misunderstand us. I really just wanted to apologize to you. We work at the same company and I really don't want our work relationship to go south just because of some misunderstanding." Anderson adds.

"How about we all just sit down and talk first and if you want to leave, we can after we listen to him. I mean, he is right. You guys are working together at the same company. You should clear everything up." Nadia advises.

"Thank you." Anderson tilts his head down at Nadia.

"You're welcome." Nadia grins.

"This is for you. I hope you can accept a sincere apology." He moves the margarita glass in front of her, calling the bartender to give Nadia another glass.

Sia eyes him suspiciously.

"I swear I didn't know you would be here. You can ask the bartender. I opened a karaoke room before you even got here." He explains. "We can move there it has a little privacy."

"Yes, that'd be nice. Sia, c'mon, let's go." Nadia gestures.

"What, is he paying you to pursue me or something, Nadia?" Sia asks angrily.

"No! No, I've never met him before. Are you nuts? He just... seems really sincere. Also, you shouldn't just accuse him without any evidence.

What if he really didn't do it?" Nadia tries reasoning with her. "Let's go!" Nadia pulls her friend's arm inside the private karaoke room.

For some reason, something told Sia this wasn't a good idea. However, she has no choice but to follow Nadia and Anderson to the room. There are two other girls and a man inside the karaoke room. The girls immediately give Sia a weird look which makes her feel a bit uncomfortable while the other man seems more friendly and his singing voice is nice so it isn't hard for Nadia to get cozy with him right away. Anderson introduces them as his web marketing employees.

"Now do you believe me yet? I didn't follow you here, you see. This is really just a simple coincidence." Anderson repeats. "But I am really happy to see you here. Do you come here often?"

"I haven't been here for while." She answers while scooting away and keeping her distance from the guy.

Suddenly Sia feels her phone silently ringing. She looks at the screen and the word 'Bossy Boss 'shows which causes her mood to shift spontaneously. She hurriedly picks up the phone and walks out of the room.

"Hello..." Sia yells to make her voice louder than the scene at the bar.

"Where are you?" Eli answers back.

"I'm with Nadia."

"I'm going to send Jace to pick you up." Eli commands. Jace had told him he sensed that something wasn't right but he wasn't sure what it was.

"Um, no... why? He doesn't need to come." Sia insists "I'm okay, really."

"This isn't a choice, please, just tell me where the two of you are." Eli asks again slowly.

"I'm with Nadia. Will you come to work tomorrow? Your office is already done and it looks nice. I thought you would come and see it." Sia has many things to tell Eli but the pub music was too loud.

"I will go and see you tonight. Where are you?" Eli needs a clear answer, getting more frustrated with every moment.

"Sia...you good?" Nadia comes out of the room, calling Sia back.

Sia flashes Nadia a quick okay gesture," I gotta go. I can't hear you very well anyway. Hope to see you tomorrow, boss!" She says before quickly hanging up. Her face smiling without knowing it.

"You look happy." Anderson states surprisingly after Sia returned to the room.

"Oh it's nothing." Sia shakes her head.

"Your drink started to melt so I ordered you a new one. Nadia said you prefer red wine." Anderson hands her another glass. "Are you still angry with me?" He asks.

"Doesn't matter. We're coworkers anyway and I hope our relationship will stay that way, hm? Also if you could please have the website take down that article I will really appreciate it." Sia states in a business like tone.

"I will do that first thing in the morning." Anderson promises. "Let's finish this glass and after tonight, I promise to behave myself. I will no longer cause you anymore trouble." He smiles.

"Thank you. I better have your word." Sia raises her glass, sipping it gently.

"Who was calling you anyway?" Anderson points at her phone.

"My dad. He wants me to go home early." Sia says.

"It's not even midnight yet. You tell him that you're with me?" He pours her another glass of red wine.

"No...no...I don't want anymore. Tomorrow my boss may come to the office. I don't want to be hungover" Sia refuses.

"Your boss? That man, Eli?" Anderson's voice becomes rough as he mentions Eli's name. "You're with me tonight, no one can say anything. Your dad told me to take you out more often too." He boasts while putting his arm around her. Sia feels that something is wrong but she doesn't have the energy to swing his arms off from her shoulder. She now feels as if the room is spinning, causing her head to fall on his arm helplessly.

"Nadia..." Sia tries to call her friend but Nadia didn't hear her because she was still signing a favorite song with Anderson's workers.

"This... this isn't right." Sia thinks as she begins screaming Eli's name in her head.

Now all she is hearing is Anderson's voice laughing and she sees him taking a selfie picture with her in his arms. Then the whole room turns dark.

.....

"Sia...Sia..." Someone is calling her. Sia opens her eyes and sees Eli's hand rubbing her face trying to wake her up.

"Sia...wake up!" Eli shouts louder. Sia's eyes flick open and this time she sees Jace punch Anderson in the face so hard that she thinks she heard a 'popping 'sound from his nose.

"His phone..." Sia tells Eli. "He took my picture." She begins to remember.

Eli grabs Anderson's phone and with his hand, he smashes the phone on the table. The phone is obliterated.

"Good." Sia smiles, peacefully closing her eyes knowing that her alien boss is here and she'll be okay.

CHAPTER 8: LOVER VS FRIEND

This was yet another occasion when Luke's plan failed because of Eli. The one time he thought his planning was perfect. Luke persuaded Anderson, his playboy friend, to get involved with Sia. He told Anderson everything he needed to know about her. Who her close friend was, her favorite 'go to 'places, and her weakness. He even schemed up the marriage idea and ran it by his adopted father and David thought it was a good idea and agreed to it. If Eli hadn't showed up that night, the news about Sia would upset David and he will force her out of the house to marry Anderson.

"It's too bad, I really liked you, Eli" Luke mutters to himself, shaking his head. Eli is definitely good looking and very intelligent, anyone would know upon meeting him. Luke would rather be in Sia's place working beside him but now that seems to be impossible. Eli is too attached to Sia, Luke blames it on fate. After he found out about the Star project, he stayed up days and nights and spent countless hours working on the proposal that David offered to Eli and Eli picked Sia as his assistant, after meeting her only once. That was a big blow to Luke's ego. But he was not done yet. He now realizes that in order to get rid of Sia, he must get rid of Eli first...

.....

Sia slept the whole day after being admitted at the hospital. Eli stationed himself next to her bed as her personal guard. David came to check on her once and swiftly went back to work. Before he left though, he thanked Eli over and over for saving his daughter's life. Anderson is also at the same hospital under police watch. He has a broken nose and will require facial reconstructive surgery. David had filed a police report against Anderson for assault by administering her with an illegal substance.

There's no news about Anderson getting punched in the face but it's a good thing there is none, although Sia would enjoy hearing about it. She didn't want to be in the same headlines with him again anyway. The prior articles were taken down by David. He also demanded that the website issue an apology to his daughter and its' subscribers. David also asked Anderson to resign his job with Young Enterprise and to step down as its executive board director. Anderson was still a shareholder but he was forbidden to walk into the Star enterprise main office without a letter of invitation.

"Do you want to see your new office anytime soon?" Sia asks Eli when he come to pick her up from the hospital.

"I'll drop by tomorrow." Eli answers softly.

"I'll wait then." Sia's voice is full of happiness.

The next day, Sia orders a cake from the hotel restaurant and asks Lynn to get some balloons and colorful decorations to hang in Eli's office. Some employees who have not met Eli are more excited than the rest.

"Finally, we will get to meet him." They have heard over the years that Eli was a gorgeous man. Eli is not only handsome, but he also has a drop dead gorgeous body. He usually spends at least an hour at the gym or at a park running every day no matter how busy his schedule is.

With a newly redesigned exercise room at the Airport site, Eli starts visiting more often, and so do his female employees.

"Do you think our boss is gay?" A woman whispers.

"Here comes more daily gossip." Sia sighs.

"Yeah, he's not married yet. I wonder why…" Another adds

"How do you know that he's not married?" Lynn asks.

"He doesn't wear a ring, haven't you noticed?" The gossip gets intense.

"Shush!" Sia says, waving her hands in a downward motion to have the women lower their voices.

Eli had called earlier and explained to her that he would be a little late. He was waiting for a new guest to arrive and would personally drop her off at the Airport hotel before going to the office. Sia checks with the reservation counter to make sure that the new guest's room is set and ready.

"Ms. Young, the boss is coming." The bellboy signals Sia.

Eli walks in with a very beautiful lady who is about the same age as Sia but a lot taller like a model. She has long red hair and blue eyes. More importantly, she seems to be very close with Eli. They're holding hands, walking toward the check in counter together.

"Good morning!" Sia bows to her boss and his guest.

"Good morning. Sia, this is Jayna Cage. Jayna, this is Sia. She is our general manager here. If you need anything and I'm not here, you can contact her anytime."

"Nice to meet you, Ms. Cage. Do you need help with your luggage?" Sia asks politely.

"It is okay Sia." Eli answers. "I'll take it up for her. Can you get her key card for me?" Eli asks.

"Of course." Sia nods and walks to the check in counter. The receptionist hands Sia an envelope with the key card inside.

"Here it is." Sia gives the envelope to Eli. "WiFi instructions are in the envelope. Thank you very much and enjoy your stay." Sia says to the guest. The girl just gives Sia a grin and walks away with Eli.

"Who is she?" Everyone at the check in desk looks to her like Sia can answer all of their questions. Today was her first time meeting Ms.Cage as well.

"Mr.Star has never checked in for a guest before. Normally Jace does that, right? Strange. Is she already familiar the boss?" The receptionist wonders.

"They were holding hands so…" Housekeeper chimes in.

"Does Eli have a girlfriend on his planet?" Sia also starts questioning her thoughts. He has never mentioned any girl or lover before. Besides, even on Earth, lots of ladies have eyes on him, he is hardly involved with anyone. But then...the Star people live a very long life. Is it possible that Eli has an alien girlfriend he visits on his return to Star? Jayna does seem to be very close to Eli. Perhaps she really is his girlfriend. Sia's brain is filled with questions. "Drop it, Sia. It is none of your business if Eli has or doesn't have a lover." She reminds herself.

It takes Eli nearly two hours to see Jayna off to her room. "Have you known Jayna before?" Sia couldn't 'drop it 'as easy as she thought. Right after Eli walks into his office, she asks.

"Yes, we grew up together." Eli acknowledges before intentionally changing the topic. "Let's go have a nice lunch outside, shall we?."

"I thought the two of you would have lunch together since you haven't seen her for awhile." Sia forces her smile.

"Nope. In fact, in Star time, Jayna probably saw me like two days ago. She'll be fine without me." Eli teasingly smiles.

Sia doesn't want to sound like a jealous girlfriend because plainly she's not his girlfriend. Yet she doesn't know why she felt the urge to know what their relationship to each other if any. "Who is she? Can you tell me just so we know how special we should treat her?" Sia walks closer to him and stares at his face the way he does to her.

"She is my umm…'heavenly mate!' Yes." Eli stammers after some time carefully choosing his words to explain his complicated relationship with Jayna.

"A what?" Sia raises her voice.

"Shhhh…" Eli covers Sia's mouth. "We have never copulated…" He whispers in her ear while holding her in his arms to make sure she doesn't freak out. "We've been matched as a couple so we can reproduce but I absolutely have no intention of having a baby with Jayna."

Sia tries to take his hand away from her mouth so she can talk.

"Promise me first that you won't get mad or yell at me." Eli says.

"Umm…" Sia nods.

Eli slowly releases his hand and lets Sia go.

"So… she's your fiancé basically." Sia asks. She has a disappointed look in her eyes.

"I think humans would call it that, but for us, the concept of matching is very different. Star people are matched by an Oracle machine called 'Stargazer' based on our personal information such as genetics, emotion, lifestyle etc. There is no love, no family involved whatsoever. We do this to make sure that we will have the best genetic outcome for our offspring. But I don't need a baby and I don't want to do anything with Jayna. I lived here most of my life and Jayna lived on the Star planet most of her life. There is no way we can raise a child together. Do you understand?" Eli explains as basically as possible.

"But she followed you here to earth!"

"It doesn't mean anything. I don't want to mate with her and I don't have to. She cannot force me and I cannot force her to do anything. You see, for the Star people, we don't love. A couple relationship is formed strictly for reproducing so as to expand our race. Love for the Star people is meaningless, a silly thing and that is why I find the human race so special. Expression of emotions is an integral part of the human world. Emotions such as hate, love, and anger. Those emotions are purely human but the Star people are not allowed to possess emotions. Eli carefully conveys his thoughts into words because he didn't want to hurt Sia's feelings.

After listening to Eli justifying himself, Sia turns away and smiles to herself thinking...Why does her boss have to be this cute!

"Then why is Jayna here?" She adds another question.

"I don't know but most Aliens come here for leisure." He sighs, "Now, Miss, can we get something to eat now? I haven't had time to eat this morning and I am starved."

Aliens have used the Oracle Machine to find their mates long before humans have. They live longer than humans. They don't date. They don't cheat. They don't have couple fights. No wonder they got bored and came to earth...

.....

Six months later, Jayna becomes a model for several fashion magazines. It is inevitable that she will become popular. After all She was gorgeous and she had alien connections in the fashion industry. Jayna travels a lot but when she was not traveling, she often mingled with Eli at his office all day which made Sia uncomfortable. The only time Jayna did not attach herself to Eli is when he had to be in a meeting. So, Eli started scheduling meetings all the time. Right now Eli started discussing his interest in a long term investment plan and partnership with Young enterprise. This new agreement must be finalized before the rent contract at the Airport hotel ends. Since David knew that Eli had started working on a long term investment proposal with Young Enterprise, David had suddenly begun to be extra nice to Sia.

From the beginning of the deal between Young Enterprises and Star Hotels, Mr. Young had hoped Sia would share insider information about Eli's private dealings like a corporate spy. Even though Sia is privileged to Eli's plans, she cherishes her business relationship with Eli. She would never divulge anything to David. Sia respects Eli's trust in her. So naturally David asks Sia if she knows anything about prospective clients that Eli may be negotiating with. Normally Sia would answer her father truthfully but in this situation she let her father guess.

"Yes, of course. Because so many hotels contact him all the time, Eli wants the best deal." To Sia, she's not completely lying. What her father didn't know is that Eli was not looking to partner with other competitors because he trusts her with all his alien secrets. However, if she told her dad that, he may start taking advantage of Eli, which Sia doesn't want her father to do. Eli is not a business man. He doesn't know too much about the games and tricks that often goes on in the corporate world. All his plans are centered around assurance of survival and sustainability of the star people.

"I really hope that our partnership contract with Eli will succeed because if we can expand our hotel this time, I will nominate you to be on the Executive Board Committee. After all, you are my only child and I am hoping that you will inherit my legacy one day." David says. He has always wanted to tell his daughter this but Sia has always been the 'good for nothing 'girl before and he was always afraid that the shareholders wouldn't accept her. He now realizes that Sia has grown so much since she took on the airport hotel project.

"I hope so too, Dad." Sia smiles proudly.

.....

Jayna called Eli to run with her early in the morning. Eli couldn't refuse since Jayna is now on his VIP guest list at the hotel. "I'm soooo glad I can secretly date you every morning." Jayna intentionally says in front of Sia to make Sia mad. Jayna's sarcasm and sassiness has definitely improved since she first came to earth. Sia's glad that Jayna cannot read her mind. Otherwise, Jayna would learn so many bad words from being inside Sia's head.

"When will you go back to New York again?" Eli asks. He discards his running clothes to change into a suit because he has a meeting to attend at David's office with Sia later on.

"I want to take a long break this time. I feel like I spent too much time working and have missed my chance at being with you." Jayna answers while helping Eli put on his suit.

"Most of the people here spend their time working, Jayna. I'm also on the clock and I won't have time to care for you everyday." Eli says.

"I am your guest and taking care of me is also your job." Jayna argues.

"Which is why I hired all these employees to work and take care of my guests so that I have time to focus on other important duties." Eli stresses on the word 'important,' Jayna's face turns red.

"Am I not important to you?"Jayna demands

Eli sighs and walks to the entrance of his office, closing the door so as to seal in Jayna's voice. "I know what you are trying to do, Jayna, but we've talked about this before. I am not interested in marrying you and you really shouldn't have waited for me."

"But you cannot avoid the prediction made by the Stargazer. We are destined to be together but you keep yourself on this planet, constantly leaving me alone. That is why I have followed you here. I want to take what is mine." Jayna shouts.

"I am not yours and the prediction isn't final. I will show you that the prediction can be changed." He exhaled warily.

"Everyone knows that if you change your destiny, it will affect your life, Eli." Jayna immediately snaps at him. She learned to express human emotion faster than any alien he knew because of all drama and action from her profession.

"I don't care. From now on, I will ask my employees to tend to all your needs whatever those needs are. If you don't feel safe, I will ask Jace to watch over you while you are in New Mexico. Otherwise, please go back to New York and don't waste my time playing this silly game." Eli retorts while staring at her. "Now, please excuse me. I have a meeting to attend." Eli opens the door and waves his hand, sending Jayna out of his office.

"You will regret doing this to me!" Jayna mutters.

"I am regretting it now for not doing this sooner." Eli whispers back.

Everyone notices as Jayna storms away.

CHAPTER 9: SECRETS REVEAL

Don't underestimate love-hate relationships. Jayna came this far from her planet just to be closer to Eli but she realized that Eli was involved with a human girl again. She knew exactly what Eli felt for Sia. This is not the first time he ignored her request to consummate. Sia looks just like Anna, the girl who once captured Eli's heart and took him away from her. However, this time, she won't let Eli go that easy. As much as Jayna believes Eli humiliated her, she cannot direct her revenge at him personally but instead target the one he loves the most.

Two months after Jayna went back to New York, Jayna who seldomly accepts interviews by the press, decides to arrange a series of interviews with radio stations and newspapers. She aims to scandalize her relationship with Eli Star her beloved fiancé. She revealed multiple photos that she took with Eli that she hopes portrays their undying love for one another. Jayna told reporters that their relationship sailed into some rocky waters due to their long distance relationship. Eli is spending more time with a third person. By not revealing the name of the third person the press became even more interested in 'the mysterious lover' as Jayna intended. Not long after that, Sia's name started appearing in several media outlets fueling conspiracies that Sia is the third wheel who complicated Jayna's and Eli's relationship. To make matters even worse, Jayna confirmed via social media that Eli's assistant Sia made her uncomfortable because Eli spend a lot of time with her. Jayna's fan club erupted into a fire storm of gossip about Sia on the internet.

Now every time Sia and Eli attend a partnership meeting together at Young headquarters, Jayna's fans showed up to mock Sia. On some days the paparazzi also swarmed the hotel entrance trying to capture a story with intent to release negative press on Sia.

The entirety of it made Eli uncontrollably mad at his Stargazer matched lover.

"Jayna you really need to stop. Nothing is going to change whatever it is that you are trying to do. It only weakens our relationship." Eli hopes that she may want to preserve their friendship. After all, He and Jayna have been close since childhood. They are like family, and Eli would rather hold her in that regard if only Jayna would stop pursuing Eli as her husband.

"I tried to save your life, Eli! You can't be with her, you just can't!" Jayna screams out of frustration.

"Sia and I are co-workers, just co-workers" Eli's voice is softer. "You know me, I don't really like to think of my future. All I want to do on Earth right now is to make sure the Star people have a place to stay. I don't want you to harm Sia because she's innocent."

"Then let me talk with her." Jayna demands.

"No." Eli immediately shakes his head.

"You don't even trust me!" Jayna says in anger. Eli looks away. "Does she even know that you have feelings for her?"

"It doesn't matter. Like I said, we are just co-workers." Eli repeats.

"Let me speak to her. I promise I will stop pestering you and leave both of you alone after." Jayna begs.

.....

The stockholders at Young enterprise are not happy with all the negative publicity about Sai, which they feared would only undermine the partnership agreement they were about to finalize with Eli. But the media's rumored publicity of Sia in a love triangle with Eli and Jayna is not only complicating things, it was potentially damaging to their prospective partnership with Eli. David had originally intended to appoint Sia to sit on the board of executives when the contract got signed. But the stockholders proposed to bar Sia from all partnership meetings to prevent anymore rumors. During the meeting to discuss the share-holders' proposal, Sia was asked to leave the room so the board can question Eli about Jayna's rumored claims on the media. Sia agreed to leave and sees Jayna waiting for her outside the boardroom.

"Hey, can I talk with you for a minute?" Jayna asks her.

"Go ahead." She sighs, it's not like Sia had any choice to refuse. Jayna had ruined her reputation, causing the board to kick her out of their meeting.

"Has Eli ever mentioned anything about the Stargazer?" Jayna starts with a question.

"Yes and he has no intention of marrying you." Sia raises her shoulders in disinterest.

Jayna shot a look at Sia before stating her rants, "Stargazer predictions are not some simple randomized motions as Eli may believe. It is our set destiny. Did he even mention what may happen by going against a destined fate?" She pauses. "He actually did this once with a girl named Anna. In the end, he left her all alone on earth and for years he lived a life worse than death. And do you know why he's so attach to you now? Hm? You know it's not love nor affection. He is fond of you because you look just like Anna, his only human love." Jayna watches Sia's reaction with her bright blue eyes. "If you don't believe me, just ask him who Anna is. He actually named his transporter after her because she helped him with its construction."

"We're not in love." Sia's once stern voice begins to crack

"That's good because I want him back." Jayna narrows the space between them, intently staring at Sia.

Sia turns away from Jayna, and sees Eli standing there looking at her, worrying. "Sia!" He calls her name softly and reaches out to her but Sia completely avoids him and runs away.

"What did you say to her?" Eli is displeased with Jayna.

"The truth." She answers with a satisfied smile. He grits his teeth forcing himself to stay calm before chasing after Sia.

Jayna's fans crowd the buildings entrance so Sia sneaks out from the back, Eli follows her through a back alley.

"S-Sia...." Eli calls after Sia which makes Sia run even faster to get away from him. She encounters a car, driving at a minimum speed, and assumes it'll will stop while she sprints across the road, instead the driver accelerates straight towards her.

"Sia! Look out!" Eli shouts. His reflexes are much faster than the average human, He uses this to his advantage by jumping in front of Sia, the car crashes into him before it comes to a halt. Half of the car is broken into pieces clearly the driver is okay from the way he bolted from his car. Once again, Sia finds Eli covered in blood.

"God, Eli! Are you okay?" Sia asks.

"I'm okay. Let's go." Eli answers and before an ambulance comes, he takes Sia's hand and runs towards the opposite direction, leaving the accident scene with no one present.

Lurking behind the scene, Luke's jaw drops with surprise as he just witnessed this unbelievable incident. "What is he?" Luke may finally have the leverage he needed to discredit Eli.

.....

Before telling Jace anything, he had telepathically sensed Eli's injury already. Eli's right arm is bleeding profoundly because he used it to block the car from hitting her. This time Sia knew that she cannot call for help because he can't be treated at a human hospital as she learned from the previous accident. The only thing she can do is hide him somewhere to protect his identity and wait for Jace to come and find them.

"Your body is very hot. Are you sure you're okay?" Sia is concerned even though she has been told that Aliens cannot die from any bodily injury.

"It's a reaction to the healing process. It is similar to when humans get infections and the body swells or heats up, it's simply a response. It is just that we heal faster than humans so we generate more heat. Don't worry, Sia." Eli closes his eyes. He breathes faster than normal because of the pain. "I'm okay."

It doesn't take very long for Jace to arrive. He takes Eli back home which is not far from where they were. Jace knows how to apply first aid to Eli's injury. From how efficiently he got to work he seemed very experienced at this. Similar to treating humans, Jace stops the bleeding first. "The more he bleeds, the longer it takes his body to heal." Like Eli told her before, they can't use medication intended for humans. If aliens are injured on earth, they just need to let their body heal on its own. The longer the healing process, the longer he must experience pain.

"Your arm is broken." After cleaning up the wound, Jace can now see Eli's bone underneath the skin. Eli nods. Jace offers him a gauze pad. He bites on it and Jace starts resetting the bone back in place. Eli screams in agony through the gauze. Sia closes her eyes, a painful feeling welling up in her stomach and throat, hearing Jayna's voice yelling at her, "How many times do you want to hurt him?"

"I want to go home." Sia says after Eli's wound is bandaged.

"Please don't go." Eli begs. He tries to get up. When he was in the meeting, the executive board wanted him to consider hiring Luke as his assistant to avoid any more bad press. He declined to accept their suggestion so now the last thing he wants is for Sia to run away from him too. Sia stared at him for a long time until her tears came streaming down her cheeks. She tilts her head up to stop the tears, instead her tears flow uncontrollably.

"A-Anna… tell me everything you know about her… everything. What did she look like? What did you do together? How did you feel when you were with her? I want to know it all!"

"Sia, this might not be a good time." Jace's main concern is to treat Eli's injury. Jace knows how traumatizing that whole emotional event was for his friend and he didn't want Eli to relive that traumatic episode while his body needed to heal.

"It's okay." Eli assures Jace, offering his left hand. Jace doesn't look happy but this is Eli's decision and he needs to respect it.

He takes Eli's hand and opens his other hand to Sia's. Instead of telling Sia the story, Eli has Jace conduct his memories to her using Jace as a conduit.

Eli had met Anna when he traveled to Scotland. She was the daughter of an inventor and engineer. A rare women that was educated from a young age. She learned mathematics, chemistry, and mechanical principles from her father. When she was only 18 years old, her father tried to arrange a marriage to one of his friends but she refused and ran into Eli who was traveling the earth. Eli was also supposed to marry Jayna per the Stargazer prediction but instead he followed Jace to earth. Jace had already traveled the earth many times using his spacecraft and had more experience living on earth than Eli. To this day, Jace still doesn't know if his decision to bring Eli with him was a good idea.

While Jace and Eli were about to fly back to the Star planet, their spacecraft unexpectedly underwent a technical malfunction. Anna helped them find engine parts. In a very short period of time she learned the spacecraft's technology. Later on Anna and Eli had developed their relationship and they decided to create a machine that would transport Star aliens between earth and the Star planet at speeds not previously possible by any known vehicle. The space travel machine was a success and named it 'ANNA'. To test the machine, Eli had to go back to the Star planet alone. In order to return to earth, Eli still had to build another ANNA to send him back to Earth. Unfortunately, it took Eli longer than he expected. When he returned to earth he realized that Anna had died from tuberculosis five years before his return...

Sia opens her eyes. Eli's eyes are still closed and tears trickled down his face nonstop. His emotional pain is obviously worse than his physical pain and now Sia understands why Jace didn't want Eli to revisit this event.

Many say that aliens can't cry. Evidently they are capable of crying. Sia knows now that phenomenon is untrue. That the loss of a perceived significant event may trigger an emotional response as powerful as that experienced by Eli.

CHAPTER 10: I WON'T GIVE HIM UP

Love is suffering. That's why the Star people ultimately decided to suppress love and to use the Stargazer to bring their people together. Love is the most heartbreaking emotion that one can posses. Waiting to love, waiting for love, waiting to be loved. Once people learned to love, it becomes even more painful to live without it.

"Forget the past, live for today, and don't think about tomorrow. One day at a time," is the best motto Sia decides to hold onto. She's willing to be anything for Eli, his assistant, his lunch friend, his exercise partner, or his 'Anna' as long as she can bring happiness back into his life.

"You have no self-respect. He doesn't see you for yourself, he only sees his previous love. Don't you get it?" Jayna glares at her with disdain.

"At least he looks at me," Sia strikes back, "You may have travel far to pursue him but he still rejects you daily. I wouldn't be so proud if I were you." Sia shrugs and glances at her watch. "Oh, my sincerest apologies but I must check the kitchen before my boss comes. If you need anything else, please let a concierge know." Sia deliberately switches to manager mode, bowing her head to Jayna. Sia decides it was fruitless to argue with Jayna.

Jayna was defeated. Her desperation and final attempt to chase off Sia had failed. But she had to stop because she had promised Eli that she would stop all the press attempts once she spoke with Sia. Keeping her promise, she put a stop to the negative and untrue media coverage.

Jayna took the next flight back to New York to continue with her work. Since then, she hasn't mentioned her relationship with Eli again, her fan club quickly forgets his name.

Eli signs a partnership contract with Young enterprise to expand the Airport hotel in exchange for 75 percent of the hotel sales. The name of the hotel was changed to Meelan Hotel, "Meelan" meaning union. He wishes to expand this hotel and open it to both aliens and humans. He has never opened his hotel to humans before because humans had more needs than aliens and he was not familiar with all their needs. Now, with Sia's help, he wanted to give it a try.

On opening day, half of the newly added wing was already fully booked. Sia recommended the special themed rooms for guests with specific tastes such as South Western style, Adobe style (an idea she got from Carls's home, the hidden Indian village near Chaco Canyon), and an Alien themed decor which Eli complained was far from how aliens actually lived but the kids love it. Sia had a projector installed to display the constellation, such as those used a planetarium.

"We should watch the real night sky together." Eli holds Sia from behind while placing his chin on her head.

"Don't do that! The employees will see us." Sia takes his arm off her shoulder.

"There's nobody around here, Miss Young. Look at the time!" Eli raises his wrist for Sia.

"I regret expanding the hotel because now we don't have time to go anywhere anymore."

"Oh?" She peeks at Eli's watch, seeing that it is nearly ten. "Oh, my goodness!" Sia jumps, finally noticing how dark it is outside. Earlier, she was excited about her dad's nomination to appoint Sia to sit on the executive board for Young enterprise. She was just trying to clear her desk of the work she was tasked to complete, thinking this is a good opportunity to learn to work at the policy level and to lookout for anything that relates to Meelan Hotel in case the topic arises.

"Hey, how about we go watch the stars together at my house?" Eli says suddenly. Sia has been to his house only once when he got hit by that car to protect her but at that time she was too worried to bother looking around. All she remembered was that his house was on top of the mountain. The house itself wasn't very big but the property was wide with lots of big trees.

"I thought you don't take visitors there." Sia teases.

"It gets lonely without human interaction." Eli flirts with her, tugging on her sleeve. Sia immediately moves away. Eli flicks her forehead with his index finger and smiles. "Actually, the pantry does need to be restocked and a good cleaning is in order too. Come and help me." He changes his voice. "Let's go! It's Friday night! I heard humans don't like working on Fridays anyway."

"Who said that?" Sia laughs and lets him pull her away. Sia is beginning to love this bossy version more and more.

At the house, the pair stocked Eli's refrigerator with enough food to keep them locked up for weeks. He actually plans to keep Sia for the weekend as he noticed how hard Sia was working the week of the grand opening and he doesn't want her to worry about work anymore. Eli asked Jace to cover her work this weekend and even paid Lynn overtime to help Jace while Sia and him get away from running the hotel.

There's a swimming pool in the back of Eli's house along with some lounge chairs which offer a comfy view of the starry night sky. Sia's eyes glimmer at the sight of the stars, unobstructed by artificial city lights.

"Can you see your planet from here?" Sia asks.

"No." Eli shakes his hand. "Even with a telescope, we still cannot see it from earth."

"I wish I could go to your planet." Sia yawns while closing her heavy eyelids.

"I wish you could too." Eli mutters, placing her head on his shoulder.

Sia woke up later in Eli's guest bedroom, a stack of her clothes for the day sat on a hardwood dresser with a post-it note in messy handwriting saying, "Good morning! I'm cooking right now, so come out when you are ready. - Eli"

Walking towards the dining room, Sia's eyes widened, "Wow…" All the food on the table made her stomach ache. Huevos rancheros, cheesy enchiladas, and a stack of steaming flour tortillas decorated the table. Glistening, silky, red chile sauce sat in a bowl just waiting to be served along with a saucer of green chile which smelt of roasted sweet candy. A pitcher of orange juice sparkled in the sunlight, reflecting the dancing rays of sunlight. Sia never sat down so fast for a meal in her life. "I didn't know you could cook…"

"I once heard a woman say that a man looks sexy when he cooks so it motivated me to learn." He jokes. Actually, most aliens have a lot of time to learn such skills since they have a long life span. For him, the longer he stays on earth, he learns a human skill that he perfects to the level of an expert. Learning human culinary arts was one of the first skills he picked up.

"You look sexy just standing still, Mr. Star." Sia bats her lashes, "How lucky to be an alien! You don't even have to try that hard to please a woman."

"Umm… well, that's is good to know I guess." He chuckles, placing a plate of food in front of her. "If that's the case, perhaps I can take you on a date later today?" Eli asks with his soft voice.

"Hm? Where?" Her eyes shine bright.

"Can't tell you yet. You'll see." He smiles.

After a satisfying breakfast, Eli drove her out of town deep into the mountains. A man waves at Eli as the car approaches. Eli stops the car to cover Sia's eyes with a blindfold.

"Don't peek!" He commands.

Eli gets out and comes back 10 minutes later to get her out of the car. All Sia can hear is a very loud sound of air blowing from the sky. After uncovering her eyes, she realizes the loud blowing sound was in fact a hot air balloon. He even hired a balloonist to pilot the balloon and take them on a private tour, a service not many tourists know they can charter.

"Oh my god..." Living in New Mexico, Sia had seen balloons before but she never had the chance to ride on one because she was afraid. However, she won't be afraid today because Sia always feels safer when Eli is with her. They've been though what seem like everything that could go wrong: an elevator accident, a car accident, a crazy jealous alien fiancé. Throughout it all, nothing has happened to Sia. If today, she were to sky-drive, she would not be afraid so long as Eli was right next to her.

"Let's go!" Eli lifts her up and sets her down in the gondola before he hops in. The balloon slowly rises off the ground, Sia instinctively grabs his arm tight. She bets Eli is probably thinking this height is nothing compared to seeing earth from space.

The air is colder at this elevation she observes, wishing she wore a bigger jacket. She begins shivering so Eli wraps her in his jacket.

"You cold? I'm sorry, I forgot to tell you," he rubs her hands in between his.

"Where are we going anyway?" Sia asks. The balloon seems to be traveling toward the mountain into another town.

"It'll just loop around the river and come back." Eli coughs harshly while answering her question. His brows furrow before smiling at her like nothing happened.

"Are you okay?" Sia has not seen Eli cough before so it sounded strange to her. "You should take your jacket back." Sia thinks the cold wind may be the cause.

"No, I'm fine. You wear it." He hugs Sia's body instead. "Now I'm not feeling so cold anymore." He winks. Sia feels her face blush and this time, it isn't from the cold.

After the balloon tour, Eli took Sia to a jewelry market in Santa Fe where they end up eating the best street food Sia has ever tasted before driving back to Eli's house.

Eli grills the meat he bought yesterday for dinner. Not to his surprise, Sia doesn't know how to cook because she had her meals prepared and delivered to her daily by the hotel chief. "You really are a good chef." Sia's mouth waters from the smell of the sizzling steak. Candles on the table, no music, outside by the pool, a slight breeze sways past, Sia tucking a loose strand of hair behind her ear as birds chirped their melody. Picture perfect, like a scene from a romantic movie.

"You should move in you know, I can cook for you everyday." Eli sits at the opposite side of the table, putting his plate down.

"W-What did you just say?" Sia is stunned. Eli frequently jokes around with her all the time, she doesn't know if he's being serious or joking half the time.

"Marry me." His voice is clear this time. He takes out a ring, one that must've been from Santa Fe. "This... this is how they do it on Earth, right?" He has never proposed to anyone before, even with Anna. Looking at Sia's face, he starts feeling nervous.

"WHAT. Wait…" Sia is too shocked to move, or even blush. She stares at him in silence before realizing this was real. "Y-Yes…yes!" Sia exclaims excitedly without hesitation, "This is exactly how earthlings do it. This is perfect!" Sia gets up and puts her face closer to Eli. He does the same and just as they're about to kiss, Eli knocks over a glass of wine, breaking the silence as they begin to laugh.

.....

David advises Sia to attend the board meeting today. Eli goes with her as they plan on telling David about their engagement. At the same time though, Eli doesn't trust Luke. He found out from Jace that Luke was behind the last car accident. They couldn't file a police report because Sia and Eli fled from the accident scene as did the assailant. While David was very happy with the good news, Luke was not. He has been receiving demanding phone calls from Mason, the driver he hired to run over Sia.

"I need the last payment." Mason demands.

"You have the nerve to ask ME for money when you didn't finish your job? I hired you specifically so that I wouldn't have to hear her annoying voice ever again and yet she's still breathing! Not only that, she was just appointed to act as the co-CEO today. TODAY! How… how can you expect me to give you a dime more?" Luke grits his teeth. It's clear now that his father won't hand over the company to him, despite his years of hard work.

"My car was towed and I can't pick it up and now I lost my job. I really need that money." Mason begs.

"Look, I will give you another job. One. Last. Job. This time you have to succeed and I will pay you what I owe you plus more because you may need to hire more people to help us this time." Luke is desperate but he has a plan.

.....

Eli's cough is getting worse. His thirty years is approaching too fast. Jace secretly took Eli back to talk with Carl who lived past his thirty years. It's very rare for a Star descendent to live longer than thirty years old even if they're born here not unless they are half human. However, when a Star person marries a human, their child will start losing their extraterrestrial abilities and eventually just become human. Human genes are dominant genes when mixed with those of an alien.

"You should go back to your planet. It's not too late." Carl advises Eli. "You don't belong here."

'I want to live as long as I can." Eli insists. He feels fine right now. His cough comes and goes but it doesn't bother him as long as he isn't exposed to wind and areas with elevated pollen.

"It will only get worse. When it comes to the point where every breath feels like sharp needles sticking your lungs, you'll begin to regret your decision. I witnessed my parents' death by suffocation. They didn't have the choice of going back to the Star planet. Unlike you, earth was their home. But you, you can always go back to Star Planet and you should go."

"How did you survive? You lived past the deadline." Eli asks.

"You wouldn't want to do what I had to do. Consistently using herbal treatments only to permanently lose most of my senses. I can't see, I can't hear as clearly as I used to. When people talk to me, I read their minds instead of listening to them. My tongue can no longer taste. You will become neither human nor alien. Again, I do this because I don't have any other choices but you do."

Aliens cannot benefit from modern human medicine. No matter the treatment, human medicine is toxic to aliens. The only way for Eli to cope with his sickness is to use herbal medicine.

"I want to try, please. What will relieve my symptoms? I'll do anything, I'll take anything." Eli begs. He doesn't want Sia to worry when his symptoms start attacking him.

"I can try but like I said, you will eventually start losing your senses. A process similar to that of human decay. It won't be very long."

Eli nods. If this is his fate he will accept it. He already has done so many things in his life. Staying with the person he loves is the only thing he has not attempted and would very much like to achieve.

Carl gives Eli a box of herbs. Carl knew Eli would need it soon so he had it prepared in advance.

"I don't feel good about this." Jace shakes his head unsatisfied with his friend's decision.

"You can feel anything but you cannot tell anyone. This is my personal choice and I hope you will honor it as it is a personal matter to me."

Their drive back to the city was long, especially now that they had nothing pleasant to talk about, so they kept their thoughts to themselves.

CHAPTER 11: OLD ENEMY

"That was fast!" Nadia gasps as Sia gives her the wedding invitation. "Oh my God, you are really out to break a girl's hope, you know that right?" Nadia jokes.

Sia rolls her eyes and smirks, "We're not fast, Robert and you are just slow." Besides, Sia now knows Eli has only so much time to live on earth that she wants to spend as much time with him as she can.

The wedding reception is planned to take place at the Meelan Hotel. At first Sia wanted to host it at the Star hotel with the beautiful view of Downtown but Eli's afraid of a repeat lab incident so he didn't agree to it.

"You'll be my bridesmaid, right?" Sia asks Nadia.

"Bridesmaid? Of course! You already know I'd do anything for you. You want Harry Styles and Beyoncé at your wedding? Consider it done."

"Imagine," Sia chuckles, "No, I actually want to keep it small but I think my dad has already planned a grand wedding for me. Of course, most of the guests being from my dad's side. Eli didn't invite anyone other than Jace." He had also invited Carl and his assistants but Carl turned down the invitation. Eli said he hasn't been outside of his village for a while and it may be an inconvenient for him to attend.

Luke, on the other hand, is extra helpful when it comes to helping out. His skills as a planner really came through and their father was quite impressed.

Although, Eli is not human, he observed all the rules and making of a wedding ceremony without a single compliant, sharing a few words about each other, exchanging vows, and Eli's favorite part, kissing.

When the time came for the bouquet toss, Sia intentionally tosses it to Nadia but her beloved friend still misses it anyway.

"A man will never propose to me, even if I did catch the stupid bouquet." She cries out, feeling defeated and stressed.

"Don't say that, who wouldn't propose to you," Sia ensures.

The limousine arrives on time and just as Sia and Eli are about to hop inside, one of the organizers runs up to Sia and explains that her father wishes to talk with her in private before she leaves.

"Why would he need to talk to me now?" Sia wondered as she followed the organizer back to the hotel while Eli is waiting in front of the limousine. He isn't worried until he sees David walking out of the hotel to send them off but Sia isn't with him.

"Dad? Where's Sia?" Eli asks.

"Eh? I thought she was with you. I haven't seen her since you guys left the reception. Perhaps she went to the restroom."

Eli raises a worried brow and runs back to the hotel, his breath growing harsh. He put his guard down today, just this once, and now he regrets it. He should've been more careful...

"Sia, she's missing." Eli tells Jace, a worried tone in his voice. "Do you sense anything?"

"No," he answers. "Have you checked her phone's location?" Jace hands his phone to Eli. Since the incident at the karaoke bar, he had asked Jace to follow Sia's phone in case something like this happened.

Checking his phone, Eli's heart nearly stops. Sia's phone is moving away from the hotel. "Get the car." Eli grips Jace's arm and makes his way to Jace's car. The phone continues to move until it finally stops at a park far north of the hotel.

"This isn't right…" Eli talks to himself. He couldn't visualize Sia or anyone for that matter and he doesn't sense her or anything that belonged to her around here. Eli decides to check the nearest trash bin by the parking lot only to find Sia's phone on top. "Argh!" Eli holds Sia's phone yelling, his skin growing red, "They deliberately lead us in the wrong direction. They know we're on to them."

"I think we should go back to the hotel and wait for them to contact us there." Jace suggests. He has more experience than Eli and he knows it won't be helpful to just drive around without a clue. Eli decides to call David to send the guests back. He hasn't told much to David other than the fact he's looking for Sia and that he's coming back now to talk with him. David agrees this is the best way to handle the situation so he announces to the guests that the groom and the bride had already left in their private vehicle.

"Where's Luke?" Eli asks almost immediately after.

"He drove back with the organizer team." David answers.

Eli recalls that when he drove the car out to find Sia, Luke was also driving out and even waved at him but he didn't think anything of it at the time. Now he wants to kick himself, Sia was in that car with Luke, no doubt.

"Do you have Luke's cellphone number?" He asks before David gives it to him. Unfortunately, Luke's phone was shut off, but that's all he needed to know. Eli shakes his head, "It must be him."

"What is going on?" David asks.

Jace informs David that he has been investigating Luke for two previous accidents related to Sia and the union coup that Luke may be involved in. David is in shock because he didn't know that he had raised a snake this whole time. David rings Luke's phone again. There still is no answer. In the meantime, Eli receives a message on Sia's phone that instructs him to go to an old property owned by Young Enterprise.

"I know that place. The renter went bankrupted so no one has been there in a long time." David's voice begins to rise, "I'm- I'm calling the police. That man better not lay a finger on my daughter!"

"No, I'm afraid he'll hurt Sia. I will go." Eli offers. "That's what he wants." He shows the message to David. "Just... just please don't call the police and don't tell anyone. I'll get her back, I promise. I don't want to alarm them because they may harm Sia. They've done it before, they can do it again."

Jace hands the car keys to Eli. "I'll follow you." Jace sends a telepathic message, Eli nods in response.

The location described in the message for Eli to go is not far from the hotel but Sia isn't there. After Eli gets out of the car, a man tells him to get into another car to make sure Eli is alone. The man proceeds to remove Eli's cellphone and checks him for electronic devices that could potentially track them. He then covers Eli's eyes before driving off slowly. Eli knows these people are criminal in nature, they've planned everything carefully in advance. Once the car left the city, the man placed a call and turned on the speaker in front of Eli. Luke's voice comes through the speaker.

"Tell your guy to stop following us." He orders and Eli hears Sia's cry. His heart rate increases immediately.

Eli grabs the phone from the man and dials Jace's cellphone. "Stop following." His voice is serious. Jace slows his car and finally turns back to the city.

It feels as if the car has been driving out of the city forever but it has only been about two hours before Eli senses they have taken a dirt road, the engine finally comes to a halt.

"Get out." The same man uncover's his eyes. His eyes adjust to the light as he spots an old workshop surrounded by scrap metal, car tires, and about three men holding metal pipes, awaiting orders. At the end of the room, Sia is in her wedding dress, dusty and torn, sitting on a small metal chair. Luke is also standing next to Sia along with Anderson, the protest leader, whose knife is pressed against Sia's throat.

"You really came." Luke observed in a twisted smile. He still doesn't understand what Eli saw in his sister. He didn't know why Eli followed her around everywhere, to protect her.

"What do you want?" Eli never likes speaking with Luke. Even when he first met him. He found Luke's demeanor and personality unpleasant. He always felt uneasy in his stomach. But now, he knows why he never felt at ease with Luke. He was down right evil.

"Well, it's kinda too late now to get what I want. You ruined it." Luke mutters. "Now all I want to know is who you really are. When that car hit you, nothing happened. Not even a scratch. What are you? Huh? You're not human!" Luke shouts before signaling his men to attack him.

One of the henchmen grabs Eli from behind, attempting to put him into a choke hold before Eli elbowed him off with a quick and precise hit, the man backs off whimpering, with Eli heard what sounded like a crack in his ribs. His buddy quickly runs to help, a shiv in hand. He slams the alien against the wall. Eli releases a sharp cough coming as he is stabbed in the shoulder. The man narrowly missed his chest. Eli groans, but manages to knee his attacker's crotch which allowed him enough time to smash the man's head into the wall as he hit him with an adrenaline fueled punch. Anderson watches in horror, dropping his knife, dashing towards the door. With no time to loose, Eli sweeps Anderson off his feet, the coward falls face first onto the cold concrete floor, smashing his teeth.

Anderson lifts his head, blood gushing from his mouth and nose, "Please no more! I only wanted the mon-" BAM, Eli grabs what was left of the man's balding hair and smashed his face back onto the floor, blood from his shoulder mixing with that of Anderson's.

Luke watches in horror, staring back at Sia and then at Anderson's knife on the floor…

"S-Stop!" Luke's voice is clearly trembling but it is enough to stop Eli. He looks over at Luke who is now holding the knife to Sia's throat, both hands on the handle to steady his shaking arms. Before he could react, a goon slams Eli's head with a pipe as hard as he can, Eli's body immediately falling to the ground as blood rushed from his head.

.....

Eli finally awakens when he feels his arms and head being lifted by someone who is shouting, "Look! Look! The wounds! They're gone." He clenches his teeth, his head pounding, feeling like he is going to pass out again as white light begins to flood his vision. He tries moving his arms but his body is tied up with some type of chain so he cannot move around very well.

"Leave him alone!" Eli hears Sia's voice but cannot see where she is in the room.

"Sia, are you okay?" Eli manages to choke out.

"I'm fine. Don't worry about me." Sia, tied up just behind him, sounded surprisingly calm, Eli sighs in relief.

Later on Luke walks in with more men. Eli feels like he is in a freak show when everybody looks at him with amazement. He hates it. "So your wounds are healing fast, huh? Luke pulls out his knife, opens Eli shirt, and slashes through his chest. It was deep enough to feel the pain. He cries out but manages to keep his composure.

"You know, you never answered my question... what are you?" Luke grabs Eli's hair, snapping at one of his men. "Is the camera rolling? I'm going to show everyone who this sicko is. I wonder how they'll feel if they know you aren't human."

However, right after the video starts, a 'low battery' message popped up on the camera screen and the camera abruptly shuts down.

"What? I just charged it not long ago." Luke complains. "Stupid waste of money device...Hey, you. Give me your phone." Luke turns to grab another phone from a subordinate. He checks the battery bar, 60%. "Ah, perfect."

Luke turns on the screen but the phone shuts off again.

Eli smiles.

Luke stares at the screen and then at Eli, "You did that?"

"Even a ghost can do that." Eli says before he promptly snaps the metal chains that tied him to the pole. The chain shattered as if it was made of glass. Everyone watching in disbelief.

"Catch him! Don't just stand there!" Luke orders but before his men could move, the door is suddenly smashed in by a man with a big baseball bat.

"Jace!" Sia yells.

Jace grins, hurling the baseball bat right into Luke's chest. Retching as blood spurt from Luke's mouth, he stumbles back as he clutches his broken ribs. Jace saunters toward's Eli while the henchman watches in pure shock. Jace rips the pole that once tied Eli down to the ground and whacks Luke's henchman with a long swing, making a swift slapping noise.

While this was going down, Eli unties Sia from her binds and scoops her up, holding her tightly to make sure nobody could harm her anymore before walking out to Jace's car which was parked at the front.

"When did Jace get here?" Sia asks Eli. She knew that eventually Jace would find them though his telepathic signaling.

"An hour or so. Jace had been waiting outside listening for my cue. When he heard me, he walked in. I asked him to wait because I want to make sure you were safe." Eli explains.

"Those men knew that you weren't human." Sia worries.

"Jace has his way." Eli smiles at ease.

"But you said you can't make people forget what they have seen."

"There's no device that can erase the human mind without damaging their brain. But... who cares if we mess with their head just a little..."

"Wait, how?" Sia's eyes lit up, ready to learn another alien secret.

"Inject a person with pure Mescaline extracted from Peyote cactus to disarray his memory with some popular alien conspiracy so they can have a story to tell everyone." Eli laughs like it's a funny joke. To be fair, it is actually an inside joke between Jace and Eli. Sometimes they discussed a new story to replace the memory of a human that has learned too much of their existence.

Jace walks out in time to listen to Eli's and Sia's conversation. He smiles with them.

"It's all good." Jace raises his thumb.

"You guys are so mean. They'll probably be emotionally traumatized forever with your story." Sia says, rolling her eyes, hiding the fact that she also thinks it's funny knowing tomorrow Luke will start thinking he was abducted by an alien who made him undergo some type of surgery.

"They better be traumatized so they won't do it again. They don't deserve to live if you ask me." Coming out from the messy battle, Jace was clearly pissed at Luke and his men for attempting to hurt Sia and harming Eli in an attempt to disclose to the world that Eli was not a human being. When he caught Anderson helping Luke with the union protest at Eli's hotel, Anderson promised Jace that he would not get involved with Luke's evil schemes again and yet here he was, helping Luke carry out the kidnapping of Sia and Eli.

"Let them go through the human's legal process. At least David knows what Luke has done." Eli looks at Sia. Knowing that Luke wouldn't be scheming any more harm to his wife gives Eli a peace of mind.

"Did he hurt you?" Eli uses his finger to wipe off some dirt from Sia's face.

"No. But you…" Eli's white shirt is smeared with his blood, his body is still hot from the healing process. "Humans may be the cruelest of all species." Sia thinks, holding Eli's face so he could rest on her shoulder.

Eli closed his eyes, feeling a little tried, a feeling that he has begun experiencing more frequently soon after he started taking Carl's medication.

CHAPTER 12: WHAT A MAN LIKES IN A WOMAN

A woman often falls in love with a man who can protect her. Some women have fairy tale dreams of being a princess with a knight, ridding on a white horse, coming to her rescue, whenever she needed him. But what about men? What does a man like in a woman?

Sia was watching her husband as he slept the entire day, his face looked so peaceful. Not wanting to wake him up, she shifted around in bed. Sia wished she could do more for him but she didn't know how.

"He just needs to rest." Sia remembers Jace telling her the night they arrived back home. So all she can do is lay in the bed with him, gazing at his perfect face until he eventually opens his eyes.

"Hello my dear wife..." Eli purrs. Sia quickly moves her finger away after playing with his eyebrows for the past few minutes.

"Hmpf, you're finally awake." She teases in a delighted tone, "You've been asleep all day, I was worried something was wrong."

Eli pulls her whole body closer to him in a swift movement, his whole body on top of her. He roguishly smiles. "I heard you asking yourself what a man likes in a woman."

"How?" Sia's surprised. Can he read her thoughts now? But before she says anything, Eli starts kissing her as an answer. He already lost one night as a married couple, he has to make up for lost time...

Honeymoon Time

Since Sia likes seeing Eli cook, he decides to come to the kitchen without a shirt on and just starts flipping bacon and eggs. He would tell Sia he was shirtless because he just got done exercising. After awhile Sia thinks he doing it on purpose because they would end up eating in bed instead of at the dining table.

Eli's favorite thing to do is watch animated series on internet TV apps. That is when Sia found out that Eli could speak Japanese, Chinese Mandarin, German, and Russian and that he lived in those countries before. When Sia sits and watches animation with him, he would choose one with a naughty plot like the kids in one animated TV series talked about 'boobies'. It was funny but...umm!

His favorite activity is swimming because he loved to have her dress up in the sexy swim suits that he bought for her.

Sia now knows what a man likes in a woman.

.....

The honeymoon period was over. Time for Eli and Sia to go back to work. They agreed not to go anywhere far because they didn't want to waste time traveling by plane or car so they ended up staying home and eating out most of the time.

"Boss!" Lynn asks first thing in the morning. "How was your honeymoon?"

"Not long enough!" His answer makes all the envious girls in the office cry out aloud.

Eli started training Jace to take over some of his work. This meant Jace will be reporting to the office everyday now. Since Eli is no longer available, the girls were giving Jace more attention. When Sia sees Jace now, he often says, "Noisy...so noisy..." and shakes his head. Eli had told Sia that Jace hears their inner thoughts and those thoughts were all about him. Sia found that funny.

"Mrs. Boss," Jace calls Sia, "Eli asks if he can pick up Jayna from the Airport tomorrow"

"Why doesn't he ask me himself?" Retorts Sia, thinking why are they acting suspicious?

"He said if you say no, then I have to go." Jace whines at Sia's outburst, and reluctantly adds. "Jayna has been asking me to tell Eli to pick her up. She doesn't want me to pick her up and Eli doesn't want to pick her up. I don't know what to do."

"Why does Jayna want Eli to go get her?" Sia hurtles another question at the same time hoping that she didn't sound like a jealous wife.

"She's going back to the Star planet soon. She just wants to talk with him before she leaves." Jace answers.

"I'll talk with him." Sia assures Jace. However, when Sia meets with Eli, he immediately blurts out.

 "No, I'm not going to pick Jayna up." Sia wonders if Eli can now read her mind.

"I think she just wants to say goodbye to you before she leaves." This is what Sia thinks but Eli knows already that Jayna wants to convince him to go back to the Star planet to treat his fading health. Eli asked Jace not to mention Jayna's plan for Eli to return to planet Star. Jayna now wants to weigh in.

"You're my wife. Don't you feel anything about her attempts to meet with me?"

"No...? I trust you so why should I?." Sia replaces quickly sounding a bit defensive. Eli rolls his eyes.

"Just go and clear it up with her. You didn't invite her to our wedding and now you don't want to talk with her. Don't you think thats a little..." Sia tries to find the right word but Eli nods.

"Okay, Mrs. Boss, I'll go." He teases, Sia sighing at the nickname.

In the morning, Eli drops Sia off at the office and goes straight to the airport. Jayna's plane is on time and she steps out wearing Versace sunglasses and toting a large Louis Vuitton bag. She's now a walking luxury AD.

"Hey..." Eli nods, helping her with her superlative luggage.

"Thank you for coming..." Jayna looks at him while taking off her glasses. Eli doesn't say anything back. "Um, you think we could get something to eat first?"

"I really don't want another scandal." Eli answers, walking ahead of her.

"Eli, please. I promise, I won't cause anything." Her voice is soft, almost begging.

He stares at her with tired eyes, "Well... Where do you want to eat then?"

"I know the perfect place."

The two arrived at a local coffee shop, the aroma of delicate cakes and strong coffee permeated the café. A kettle whistles loudly in the distant. Eli enjoys drinking coffee with milk, a taste he developed while living in Scotland. Jayna still remembers this of him fondly.

"So, how is your wife?" Jayna places his order in front of him.

"Good." Eli nods, sipping his coffee.

She waits for Eli to say more but silence just fills the air.

"You didn't invite me to your wedding."

"I didn't want to bother you. Figured you were busy jet setting from NYC to Paris..." Eli says at which Jayna retorts.

"Don't lie to me, just say you wanted to protect her!"

"Yeah, I didn't want to hurt her feelings." He answers, lifting a brow, his skin appearing more pallid than the last time she has seen him.

After eyeing him up and down, Jayna stares back at her fidgeting hands, "You need to go back home... you are on a gradual decline to death for God's sake!"

"I'm still alive." He answers.

"Did you not hear me? You. Are. Dying. Eli. You can't even taste your damn coffee. I salted it and you haven't complained once. You have already started losing your senses." Jayna cries out through her clenched teeth.

Eli immediately stands up, knocking the café chair backwards as he grabs his coffee, dumps it onto the bin and walks out. Jayna follows close, tugging his sleeve.

"How long are you going to hide this from her? One day she'll know. Do you think she'll be happy knowing that you suffered day in and day out just to be with her? How is she going to feel knowing you died for her? Hm?"

"Everybody dies, Jayna. Even aliens eventually die. You're just going to live longer than me. So what?" Eli snaps, opening the car door for Jayna.

"But your actions are no different than that of a suicidal person."

"If you don't want to go, I'll gladly leave you here." Eli warns.

She opens her mouth but decides not to say anything that she will regret. Eli is the only man who can treat Jayna like this and she still doesn't understand why she tolerates that.

"I'll just tell your wife everything." Jayna threatens him.

"If you tell her I will personally tie you up and send you back where you came from, banning you from ever coming back." Eli mutters. This is precisely why he didn't want to meet her today.

"Jace, I swear I'm going to kick your butt when we get to the hotel." Eli sends a telepathic message to Jace.

Jace only responds with fear.

"Jace? You okay?" Sia asks as Jace's face suddenly paled.

"Heh, I'm okay, heh… heh" He smiles, swallowing a gulp of water, nearly spilling it on his desk.

.....

David has been teasing his daughter about his future grandchildren for months and now Sia finally gets to give him his wish. She has not even told Eli but since she's going to see her father at the board meeting first, her father gets to learn about the news before her husband. However, Sia planned something much more special for Eli. She sneaks back home early and prepares various recipes that she learned from the Internet. Later on, Jace drops Eli off at home.

"Wow...My sexy wife cooked for us today. Do you need any help?" Eli offers.

"Oh no! It's fine, how about you go have a shower first. I can do it." She grins, wanting to show off her domestic skills but it didn't seem to be working out very well, as the smell of burning garlic oil suddenly tickles Eli's nose. He runs to turn the gas off.

"Really! I'm okay. Just go!" She insists. Eli smiles following his wife's orders.

Once the table is set, Sia grins, "I'm sorry, it doesn't look half as nice as when you made it but I tried my best."

"I love it." Eli kisses her. "I love everything that you do." He compliments. "Thank you."

"By the way, I also have something to tell you." She makes her voice serious. "My dad told me to not eat your sushi anymore."

"Why?" Eli asks. Sia loves Sushi and everyone knows it.

"Because he thinks his grandkid won't like it." She makes her eyes big, smiling.

Eli creases his brow and finally gets it. "Are you-?"

Sia nods.

His jaw drops, excitement bubbling in his stomach as he holds Sia up in the air. He runs around the house, shouting. "I love you! I love you!" He kisses her multiple times before he realizes that he shouldn't be moving her back and forth too much so he put her back on the dining chair.

"Hurry! Let's finish eating so we can look at kid clothes together." He starts stuffing himself with food as fast as he can.

"Wait, no. It has been only a little over a month." She just learned today using two pregnancy tests. Both came out positive but still she wants to confirm it with a physician.

"So?" Eli is like that. When he wants to do something, he wants to do it right away. Sia knows his time is limited and she is too afraid to ask him how much time he has. For her, waking up with him every morning is a blessing.

Eli talked about his future baby the whole way home. He dropped by the book store and picked up every pregnancy booklet that he could find to read to her in bed.

Those books are like story books for kids to Sia. When Eli read, Sia just listened to his calm, deep voice and didn't remember a thing he read. Eli kept reading until his wife's eyes closed...

He kisses her and slowly gets up from the bed. It's time for him to take Carl's medicine. The medication helps with his cough but it causes Eli to slowly loose his receptive senses.

When he found out they were expecting a baby, his first thought was that he wanted to see the baby's face, a girl or a boy. It didn't matter. Eli put the medicine away and sits next to the pool looking at the stars. He starts coughing again. Like Carl said, without the medicine, each breath would feel like a million needles stabbing him. His cough is worsened by the wind. He uses a handkerchief to muffle the sound. Phlegm comes out bloody red. He closes his eyes and holds the handkerchief in his hand before getting up from the chair heading back inside.

"Sia!" He stares, startled. His hands gripping his handkerchief tighter. "I thought you were sleeping. When did you wake up?"

Sia doesn't say anything. She places her palms on the side of his neck for a long time and doesn't let go. She wants her teary eyes to stop running but it doesn't.

"Are you cold?" He asks after feeling Sia's body shiver.

Sia has many questions to ask him. "Are you in pain? How long have you been like this? What can I do to ease your pain?" But she couldn't say it. Since he doesn't want her to know, she won't ask him anything. Don't cry. Don't ask. She doesn't need any explanation.

CHAPTER 13: I HAVE NO REGRETS

Sia believes that if a couple can love one another, as if each day was a blessing, there would be less arguing and more appreciation. Now she understands why Eli doesn't like to argue with her. Instead, he wants to spend time cherishing her rather than fighting with her.

Everyone at the hotel refers to Sia as Mrs.Boss because they think she is in charge of the Meelan Hotel now but Eli doesn't mind.

"Our boss puts all of the men to shame." The hotel employees jokingly tease him.

Eli wakes up early everyday to cook breakfast for Sia before going to work. Around lunch time, his Outlook always reads that he's unavailable that is because he always makes time to eat with his wife. In the evenings, he waits for Sia so they could ride home together no matter how late it was. Before bedtime, Eli reads a chapter from one of the pregnancy guides to her repeatedly, knowing she cannot remember it the next day.

.....

"Jace, do you know when Eli's thirty years will be up?" Sia finally decides to ask Jace. Eli's cough is getting worse and more constant. She knew that he tried hard to suppress his cough in front of her but it was so obvious. He was in so much pain.

"You want to know the truth? He already reached it a long time ago." Eli had told him to not discuss his illness with Sia. Since she already knows, he figured it was no longer a secret.

"But... he doesn't look that old." Sia's mind began racing, she always thought she had more time.

"We don't age that fast, remember."

"What is going to happen then?" She asks anxiously.

"He doesn't want go back so..." Jace hesitates, not mentioning the herbal medication. Eli had stopped taking it anyway so it didn't matter if he should tell her or not. Eli's life is coming to an end and there's nothing else Jace can say.

Sia's eyes grew puffy, her throat tight. She shakes out her hands, thinking of how Eli could die right in front of her was unbearable. Eli's only wish is to remain with his wife and child for the remainder of his life on Earth, what did he do to deserve such a fate.

"What do you think I should I do?" Sia asks with a stern voice.

.....

Eli has been busy decorating the baby's room ever since Sia revealed her pregnancy results. Every time he buys new baby furniture, he always puts them together himself piece by piece. After going to the first ultrasound, for some reason, Eli has been spending about half an hour in the baby room alone everyday. Sia noticed that he looks happier with that routine so she doesn't question anything.

With every passing month, Eli arranges a photographer to take family photos of them and at night he's always sure to say, "I love you and your mama more everyday" before he sleeps.

By the third trimester, Sia knows that Eli's health is declining more rapidly and becoming almost unbearable for him yet he doesn't complain. Sometimes he collapses during a reading session and won't wake up until the following afternoon. However, when he gets to take a long rest like that his condition tends to get better. Since Jace had already started taking over Eli's work, Sia has managed to convince him to stay home with her until the baby is born. David agrees it's a good idea for them to take some maternity leave.

Tonight is another one of those nights when his illness becomes more prevalent. Despite his agony, he still wants to sit with her near the pool, looking at the stars outside. Sia let his hand rest on her shoulder.

"Do you regret marrying me?" Eli asks in a low voice.

"Of course not, I'm so glad we did. In fact, I would regret if I didn't spend time with you for just one day. This past year has been the happiest of my life." Sia beams.

Eli's eyes lit up, "I'm so grateful for our baby and I'm so grateful for you. I'm… I'm glad she'll keep you company when I'm gone." This is the first time Eli mentions his condition. Sia had been grudging this day because she always thought that she would begin bawling but now that he finally mentioned it, she was able to keep her sadness to herself. It may be because she had been mentally preparing for this day to come for a while now.

"You'll be fine… I know in my heart you still have a long life to live." Sia insists.

"I just want to see our baby." Eli states hopeful. Each day, whenever his chest pain flares up, he thinks about how beautiful his baby will be. Thoughts of his child motivates him to stay alive.

"You will. She'll be a beautiful girl with lots and lots of hair. Her eyes will be bright like stars. She'll cry so loud that she can be heard in another room. Most importantly, she'll be strong like you."

By month nine, the baby still didn't want to emerge. What a stubborn baby!

"Doctor, is there anything you can do to get this baby out sooner?" Sia implores impatiently.

"We can induce labor but the risk of complication is high and we may end up resorting to an emergency c-section if you're fine with it." The doctor says.

"I am fine with it." Sia answers quick. "How soon can we start?"

The doctor lifts her brow, surprised at Sia's abrupt decision. "I can ask the nurse to schedule an appointment for you."

"Yes, that'd be wonderful." Sia smiles.

It's like the baby knows that if she doesn't come out, she's going to get kicked out very soon. One day before the planned procedure, Sia was already screaming in back of the car demanding Jace to drive faster to the hospital. He has never been so scared of anything in his life. Sia's voice alone was enough to make the hair on his neck stand up. Meanwhile, Eli sits in the back of the car unfettered by Sia's screams and laughs at Jace's panic, reminding him to slow down. Having read many pregnancy books helped him understand the situation at hand.

Luckily, the baby's delivery is without complication. Sia pushes the baby out as soon as she is set up on the bed. Another perfect family photo is successfully taken inside the delivery room.

Eli stares at the first baby picture for a long time in the baby's room before inserting it in the baby album.

"Nice to meet you, Penelope." Eli writes on the baby book, a tear staining the page. At last, his wish has been fulfilled. He has never once regretted his decision to marry Sia. A saying emerges in his head, that most people on their death bed would say "they don't regret what they have done. Rather, they regret what they've never done." A sentence has never held so true to his heart...

.....

Eli walks to the living room where Jace, Sia, and the babysitter were lounging. Eli kisses his little girl, his face pale as paper.

"You feeling okay?" Sia holds his arm, whispering in his ear.

"I feel perfect." He kisses her hand and places it back on Penelope.

"Let's take her to the room." Jace helps Sia up as she leads the babysitter to the baby's room.

Eli walks off to the back of the house, coughing non stop. He sits under his 'Belle of Georgia' peach tree, attempting to distract himself from the stabbing pain. The wind is blowing strong tonight causing the petals of the pink peach flowers to fall beneath the trees. It is an amazing view. Eli had once told Sia that if she ate too many peaches, she would turn into one. So he knew Sia would be delighted eating a lot of peaches when she found out that there were multiple peach trees around his house and she was. So this place has been Sia's favorite since.

Sia strolls out of the house, smiling at Eli. Seeing Eli's hand covered in blood from his cough makes her pause for a moment, a feeling of deja vu overtaking her mind. Sia recognizes this scene as one from Carl's prediction.

"Are you in pain?" Sia asks softly, sitting next to him while holding his other hand tight.

He wants to say something but his lips cannot mutter a single word so he shakes his head as a reply so Sia won't worry too much about him.

"I'm not ready to say 'goodbye' to you yet." Sia speaks gently, looking straight into his luminous green eyes that she loves so much. "I am sorry" She kisses him before injecting him in the neck with a needle pen.

Eli gasps in surprise but before he knows what's happening, he feels his eyes closing and his arms become heavy.

"I'm sorry, but this is for the best, our only option." Jace emerges from the tree line, catching Eli before he collapses to the ground.

Jace and Sia rush Eli to the downtown lab. Jayna was there already, waiting for Eli's arrival. They places Eli's body inside the ANNA transporter, his wrist is scanned upon arrival. Jayna walks into another transporter room and does the same with her wrist. Everyone follows the procedure in a rush. They don't have much time because the anesthetic injection won't last very long. Before Jace presses the button, Sia walks inside the transporter, giving her last words to Eli.

"Please come back as soon as you can. I'll wait for you no matter how long it'll take." She kisses him, tears pouring down her face and all over Eli. Right after Sia comes out, the door closes. Both Eli and Jayna slowly fade away until there is nothing left inside the transporter.

Jace drives them back home, the car ride home is quiet except for the sniffling coming from Sia. At home, she goes into the baby room to seek comfort. Watching Eli nearly sacrifice his life so he could stay on Earth to be with his family, and the thoughts of him dying and leaving her forever had exhausted her mentally. Sia notices a diary laying on top of the nightstand next to the baby crib. This is the reason why Eli was in this room every night, Sia thinks as she opens it, page by page.

Hello Penelope, my dearest daughter:

I might not be able to talk with you in the future. I hope this diary can detail my feelings for your and your mother. I love your mother so very much and that's why I also love you and will always love you till my dying breath.

Sia sits down and starts sobbing loudly. Feeling a loss of love is the most suffering emotion for any human to endure. Now she knew how Eli felt when he left Anna behind. A sorrowful emotion unlike any other emotion in the world.

.....

The smell is nice, familiar, refreshing. Eli hadn't breathed this strong for a long time. He recalls when Jace asked him to go on a trip to earth. Jace had just inherited a spaceship from his father whom Jace had flown with multiple times before his father died. So Jace had been very confident that he would navigate the spaceship safely while taking his best friend, Eli with him.

Jayna was feeling miserable. She had been so happy before when her consultation with the Stargazer confirmed that Eli was her destined match. For Jace to take away her chance of marrying Eli caused Jayna to stop speaking to Jace since. At that time Eli, he didn't mind marrying Jayna but he said he would marry her when they both reached 500 years of age. Aliens are able to live for a thousand years at least. Therefore, Eli jumped at the opportunity to travel to Earth with Jace. In the meantime, delaying the timeline he set to marry Jayna.

No one expected that the commingle of human and alien genes was in their destiny. Aliens have always looked down on Humans as the weakest species in the whole universe. Without the help of aliens and their technology, humans would still be hunters gatherers. When Eli reached earth, he found human life beautiful. Humans were emotional beings something that aliens avoided because they see it as a flaw in genetics and the root of incompetency in humans to advance themselves technologically. The thoughts cause Elis heart to rush.

However, now, Eli is paying a magnificent price for it. Eli woke up this time and found himself in an alien hospital on Planet Star. He has been restrained to the RxMR (Prescribed Molecular Re-atomizer) since his arrival through the ANNA transporter. Jace had betrayed him once again. This time, his wife even played a role in it and allowed Jayna to accompany him to this hospital against his will. The Stargazer's prediction had been registered as an official document. Thereby allowing Jayna, his future wife, to make arrangements for his treatment including the power to have him restrained.

"When will they stop this damn machine!" Eli asks Jayna, clenching his fists disappointingly. RxMR (Primer) procedure seemed to run forever, like an eternity to him.

"You need to be on it for awhile. Just be patient. You've always been a calm person, why have you changed so much?" Jayna criticizes. Although she knew that Eli and her will never be on good terms ever again, she still wants to save his life. When Jace told her Sia wanted to send him back home and asked for her help, she agreed to follow her plan right away.

Upon releasing the four point restraint, Eli immediately drags himself up to his transporter room. Eli doesn't care how old his wife on earth is going to be. He still wants to be with her. Like Sia told him, the time she spent with him, even if it was for only one day, was happiness to her. He felt the same way.

ANNA transported Eli back to earth in an instant. Normally, Jace would be on standby at the downtown lab waiting for Eli to switch positions but this time Eli comes ahead of his schedule. Eli switched on a machine. It took a while for the machine to power up and update just like a human machine. Eli rolls his eyes. It had never taken this long before. He blames it on the slow internet speeds on earth. Right after the machine is up and running, he registers himself on earth which is the routine that he has to do to comply with alien regulatory laws so as to keep track of the number of aliens on earth.

Eli opens the lab door and finds Jace standing there with a young lady. She has long, wavy, jet black hair contrasted with her bright brown eyes. She wore a very short checked skirt, paired with platform boots and fishnets that ran up to her knees. A plain bandaid covered the bridge of her nose and pins decorated an oversized leather jacket that was tied tightly around her waist. Her red lipstick went well with the color palette of her skirt and braces.

She stares at him with an astonished look, her doe-like eyes in shock.

"Sia! Is that..." Eli shakes his head, looking at the lady in disbelief. "Wait, no... you're not Sia."

"Aha! Welcome back." Jace finally responds. "Penelope, this is your father, Eli Star."

CHAPTER 14: I LOVE YOU TO THE STAR AND BACK

"You're back" Jace counts, "It's been twenty years. You came back earlier than I expected."

"I should have known earlier that we didn't need to be on a waiting list for the RxMR Machine if we were dying. Jayna took me to an emergency room where I woke up connected to the machine." Eli had made sure that when he was back at the Star planet, he did not waste a minute to get to his ANNA transporter, even if he had to crawl out of the hospital bed to his ANNA transporter.

"Where is Sia?" Eli is anxious to know.

"She is gone." Jace responds.

"What do you mean she is gone? What happened to her?" Eli's voice is uneasy. He doesn't want to draw any conclusions. He wants to know the details as precisely as they occurred.

"It means she is not here. You should ask your daughter. She knows more than me." Jace throws the ball.

"You are killing me here, Jace. Just spilt it out." Eli shouts.

"I don't know anything much. Twenty-five years ago Sia was looking for a way to go to the Star planet. She thought that if Anna could help you develop the transporter to bring the Star people here then we should be able to transport humans to the Star planet." Jace explains.

"But that is impossible." Eli argues.

"I know, I know," Jace waves his hand, "and that's what I told her. But Sia didn't listen and she kept researching it until one day Carl showed at hotel Meelan."

"Carl? He has never left the village." Eli remarks.

"Penelope was ten years old. She was an intelligent kid. At five years old she could speak seven different languages. She could communicate with some animals and when Carl came, Sia took Penelope to live with Carl. Later Penelope came back alone to help manage the Star Hotel and the Meelan Hotel just 5 years ago. She has never mentioned or told us where Sia could be and that is why I told you to ask her."

Eli sighs in relief. At least there's no confirmation of Sia's death. He was so afraid that he would receive news of Sia's death the way he received news of Anna's passing. Eli glanced at Penelope, feeling a little bit awkward with her. He wanted to give her a big hug but he doesn't know if Penelope is upset with him for leaving her and her mother on earth.

The first day Eli is back at home, Penelope cooks for him and the food tastes horrible. Eli doesn't know who is worse at cooking, Penelope or Sia. When Sia was cooking food for him, his taste buds were already impaired so he didn't even know what Sia's food tasted like.

"Dad..." Eli looks at Penelope, surprised. After dinner, both of them sit next to the pool quietly the way Eli and Sia used to do in the past. "You keep looking at me because I look like mom, right?"

Eli smiles at her before he says, "You look beautiful, just like her."

"Mom always said I should have picked up your genes. She had always complimented you saying how you were the most gorgeous man in the whole world." Penelope's story makes Eli laugh.

"Sounds something your mother would say."

"Also, I read the diary that you left in my room," Penelope adds, "Mom also read it to me. Many times. She read it everyday until pages went missing. When I was two years old, I could remember everything she read from that diary so I pretended to read it aloud to her as though I could read very well. Needless to say, Mom was a little too impressed."

Eli laughs again, this time, Penelope smiles too. Eli pulls his daughter's head closer to him. "You're the cutest girl I have ever seen. You know that, right?" He feels at ease for the first time since he returned to earth. "I am sorry I didn't hold you sooner. You look too much like your mom that if I hugged you, I was afraid I would have ended up thinking that you were your mother instead. It was just...weird." Eli explains.

"Don't you feel like that anymore?"

"No, your personality is very different from your mother. You are very smart and funny." Eli reveals. He's glad that they worked through their awkwardness, having this conversation today. He thought it would take months for her to warm up to him but they managed to click instantly and naturally.

"Don't you want to ask me where mom is?" Penelope looks into his eyes. "Mom was right, Dad's eyes are like little stars on the planet. They're shiny and bright whenever he's happy." She thought.

"You will tell me when you want to tell me. I'm not going to force you," He answers. "Yes?" Penelope, doesn't answer, instead looking up at the sky. Eli does the same.

"By the way, tomorrow, let me cook for you." Eli offers.

"You couldn't stand eating my food anymore, could you?" Penelope squints at her father.

"No, I couldn't." He jokes with a half truth.

"Mom taught me you know."

"Your mom learned to cook from the internet, don't follow her technique." Eli's advice makes Penelope giggle.

The next morning, Eli wakes up early as usual, cooking breakfast for Penelope. Eli has to learn his daughter's routine. Penelope loves animals so she wakes up early to feed the wild birds around the house. She also has squirrels and roadrunners as her friends. Eli's glad she doesn't raise rats or tries to find cockroaches to feed her roadrunners.

"Mom always bragged that your food was good." Penelope picks up some Southwestern style scrambled eggs and puts it in her mouth. "It is not that special." She shrugs her shoulders.

"I think you ate too much of Carl's herbal medicine while you were at the village." Eli scolds.

"How do you know?" Penelope jokingly asks.

"Because you lost your taste buds."

"I heard you took his meds too." She points at her dad, giggling.

"Unfortunately, I did. I had to. Otherwise, you wouldn't be here." Eli frowns down at Penelope for making fun of him.

"No, I'm just joking. Your food is good." She rises two thumbs up for him.

"It seems like your mom told you a lot of things about me. How about you tell me more about her?"

"Oh...she talked about you all the time. Both of you have a tendency to be suicidal maniacs." Penelope rolls her eyes. "If I wasn't with her, she would've already done a lot more crazy things."

"Like what?" Eli props up his chin with one hand, listening.

"She was thinking about going through your ANNA transporter to check if you were still alive. Jace had to lock the lab door for a long time. Then she started asking Carl to give her an herb to lower her blood pressure and put her in a coffin to ship her to Antarctica where the ice could freeze her body until you came. Obviously, mom was watching too many Hollywood movies. Even at ten years old, I still knew her ideas were crazy."

"Then where is she right now?" Now Eli is worried.

"After we went through all of her crazy ideas; looking at the pros and cons, mom decided to travel around to research ways of contacting you. When she went to England, she found that British people were now into learning Buddhist meditation which can slow the aging process. Grandpa thought that was the best idea, living a healthy lifestyle and doing meditation, so he asked his friends in China to arrange a place in Tibet for mom to learn Tibetan meditation techniques."

"So your grandpa also knew..."

"Yeah...he knew everything including the reason you went missing. I mean, I am half-alien, half-human, dad. How long did you think we could keep it from grandpa."

Eli's face turns a little pale. So many things had happened when he was absent.

"Don't worry. Grandpa never spoke a word to anyone. He also doesn't want me to be bothered by any freak organization. I am his granddaughter after all." Penelope sounded proud.

"Interesting," Eli nods multiple times. This is what's best about humans, they are far from perfect but they always find a way to overcome their obstacles.

"So where is your mom?" Eli's eyes are shining bright with excitement but they turn dull again when Penelope answers.

"Actually, I don't know where mom is right now but she usually comes to see me every year on my birthday so she should be contacting me very soon." Penelope was so sure of it until she receives a phone call one week later.

"Hey, Penny, don't get mad but I can't meet with you this year." Sia's voice could be heard over the speaker phone. Penelope runs up to the pool so her dad can hear it.

"No Mom! Listen! Dad is already here, waiting for you." Penelope shouts.

"That's okay. I have Yoga classes to teach until the end of the month. Let him wait. I have been waiting twenty years for him. He can wait for me, he'll be fine. Got to go. Love you, kid. Bye." Then Sia hangs up.

Both Eli and Penelope are frozen in shock. Sia answered so nonchalantly, it was as if she isn't even fazed that Eli had returned.

"You're screwed, dad..." Penelope looks at him with pitiful eyes. "Don't worry though, I can take care of you even when you turn into an old man like grandpa." She jokes.

"I'm not a man, I'm an alien." Eli rectifies, splashing pool water at Penelope's face.

She laughs, "Looks like you are stuck with me for awhile, then."

"No, I wont," Eli is a bit disappointed. He has been waiting for her for nearly a month and now he has to wait again. There's no way he is doing that.

"Give me your phone." He gets out of the pool, grabbing Penelope's cell.

"No, Dad! You're all wet! Wipe yourself first, jeez!" She complains, throwing a little white towel on him.

Eli dials the contact but it's from an unknown number that cannot be reached.

"She calls from a public phone using a calling card."

"Who uses a calling card anymore?" Eli's voice becomes flustered.

"Well, I mean, she is on top of a mountain in Tibet, Dad." Penelope snaps her fingers.

"If she's in Tibet then Tibet we go!" Eli pulls his daughter's hand.

"Wait, no! I still have to work, just calm down. She'll come back soon." Penelope pulls her arm back, raising her hands together, praying for him to wait. "It won't be long. You have me anyway. I'm a good company, you won't be bored, I promise."

Eli closes his eyes in distress. It really seems like he cannot do anything but wait. This is his retribution, his fault for leaving her alone on earth for so long.

CHAPTER 15: I'M BACK

The problem with Eli coming back too soon is that he doesn't have a human identity, at least not yet. Some of the people who knew Eli when the hotel was established are still working and it would be strange if they saw that Eli looks more like he could be Penelope's big brother and not her father. The problem with that notion was that Sia didn't have a son.

"Just put on some make up or grow a beard so you will look older, dad. Like Keanu Reeves." Penelope winks her eye, laughing as she had heard a rumor about how Keanu's done that to appear older in order to play his real age. She always wonders if he's an alien too.

"Well, your mom hates beards." Eli reveals.

"Always because of mom." Penelope rolls her eyes, "You really are crazy in love with her."

"When you fall in love, you'll understand. Do you even have a boyfriend yet?"

"Does Jace count?" Penelope says in an innocent voice.

"You better not get too close to him." Eli scolds, sounding like an old father.

"Jeez, I'm just joking!" Penelope replies to save Jace's butt.

"Ding!" The door bell rings. Penelope runs to the door and looks through the peep hole to see the visitor.

"Speak of the devil..." She turns to tell her dad with a sly smile before opening it.

Eli points a threatening finger at her upon seeing Jace emerge from the door.

"Penelope, is your father here?" He looks up to see Eli standing in the hallway, "Sia was in a car accident on the way back home. She's in the ICU right now." Jace breaks the news grievously. Eli's eyes immediately change color. He drops everything and rushes to the car with Jace. Penelope does the same.

Couples destined by the Stargazer aren't meant to break that bond. Anyone who breaks it will face unfortunate consequences.

Eli hates hospitals. Every time he goes to one, he can feel the sadness and mourning of the spirits around, no matter which hospital, old or new. Now he feels even worse knowing that his wife is laying here somewhere in a room receiving treatment.

"They found some bleeding in her brain, she's currently in the operating room, Doctors are trying their best." David relays the message. He looks as worried as Eli.

————————

"Hello Penelope, my dearest daughter,

I might not be able to talk with you in the future. I hope this diary can detail my feelings for your and your mother…"

Sia was so happy to hear her daughter mention that her husband was back at home. She tried to finish everything she had to do in Tibet so she could finally go back home. She has not been back to New Mexico since she took her daughter out from her house because she couldn't bare to live in a home full of memories alone. Every time she saw the peach tree where Eli's last sat covered in blood, she felt as pained as he did. That day, the wind blew the wilted peach flowers all over his body. So every time she saw the falling peach flowers, she thought about him suffocating in pain.

"August, 4th: Your mother told me that she was expecting you. I'm so, so happy and oh so thankful. All of my worries vanished in a moment. It's the best feeling that I had since I married your mother. We went to buy you clothes and furniture all the while your mother kept saying, 'We don't even know if we are having a boy or a girl.'

September 20th: Your mother threw up the food I made for her. All she can eat are oranges and chocolates. I know you are going to be a sweet little girl but don't eat too much sweets. It will make your teeth hurt.

October 15th: We went for the ultrasound today. Your head is gigantic, you kinda look like a baby alien. Your mom wants to know if you are boy or girl so we can find a name for you but you didn't want us to know. The technician told us you kept crossing your leg so she couldn't see. So we just picked a name for both a boy and a girl. This was one of the rare times that we argued because I wanted a name that sound beautiful but your mom wanted a simple name that was easy to say. We'll probably debate about the name some more tomorrow or until you're born.

November 30th: I got to high-five you today. It was maybe more like a high foot to you. You kick so hard at night that your mom couldn't go back to sleep. I had to massage her legs for 2 hours before she could go back to sleep again but that's okay. I know you don't have that much room in there. I don't mind staying up late with your mother as long as you are happy.

January 1st: Happy New Year, my little baby. I'm sorry, I don't have that much energy to write. I miss you and I hope to see you soon."

Dear husband:

I've been waiting for about 20 years. I'm incredibly thankful that you're still alive. I'm sorry that we lied to you but now you know that was the best decision I made in my life. Hope to see you soon.

————————

"Sia..."

"Mom..."

"Someone is calling my name. The sound is so familiar. Who is it?" Sia opens her eyes and sees a nurse looking at her.

"Do you know what happened?" The nurse asks.

"No." Her mouth is dry so her voice hardly carried past her lips.

"You were in a car accident but you're okay now." The nurse touches her arm and writes down Sia's telemetry that she got from the monitor on a sheet of paper.

"Do you know who's the current U.S president.?" The nurse asks more questions.

Sia doesn't answer. She closes her eyes and wants to go back to sleep again.

"Mom..." Penelope calls her.

"Do you know what year it is?" The nurse asks a different question and when Sia doesn't answer, the nurse walks out and someone else comes to look at her.

"Sia..." Eli runs up to her and kisses her hand. "I missed you so much."

"Who are you?" Sia responds, taking her hand back slowly.

Eli's breathing halts, his heart skipping a beat. No... Sia has to be joking, he can't start over... he can't.

.....

"Mom, food's done." Penelope calls Sia. This is the first time Penelope prepared breakfast for her mother. Her father taught her how to do it and it actually tastes way better than before.

Sia came down in a blue dress ready to get back to being the boss of the Meelan Hotel again.

"You look nice." Penelope compliments. "Now i'm not going to call you mom anymore. I'll call you... boss instead. Every time I call you mom, someone will always say, 'I thought she was your sister.'" Penelope groans. "I don't think they understand that their compliments make me feel like an old lady."

"You think too much. Finish your food! Hurry, Dad is waiting. He will be mad at us." Sia gestures to her daughter to hurry.

"No way. Dad will never be mad at you. He loves you too much. Burrr..." Penelope sticks her tongue out like a little girl, giggling naughtily.

================The End================

EPILOGUE

###Dad and Daughter Moment###

"Hi, My name is Penelope. I am half human half alien. My father is the most handsome alien I have ever known but I look just like my mother because unfortunately alien genes are recessive..." Penelope speaks in front of her camera phone then moving it to Eli's irritable face.

"Penelope, stop taking my photo." Eli shouts at his daughter. Penelope is breaking all his rules on photographing people and aliens. She even convinced their alien guests to take a photo with her and posted them on her social media site.

"Dad, show me how you can drain a phone battery, I want to post it on my Insta. Here, drain mom's phone." Penelope throws her mother's phone into Eli's hand.

Eli waves his hand lazily.

The phone blips out!!!!

"Huh, wait! No, DAD... Not my phone. Arkkkkkk!" Sia grits her teeth.

=====================

###So what happened at the hospital?###

"Sia... I missed you so much." My father cooed.

"Who are you?"

"He's your husband." I answered, "Mom, you remember us... don't you? Your daughter, your husband?"

"My husband..." A twinkle formed in her eye, "is this gorgeous?" Mom began smiling uncontrollably.

The nurse entered the room but this time with a doctor.

"Is she going to be okay? I don't think mom can remember us."

"Oh, she'll be okay. It's just a side effect of the anesthesia, only temporary." The doctor laughed.

Even through tears, I'll never forget how bright my father's eyes became as he held both of us in his arms for the first time.

========= Really! The End =========